Acting Edition

Death by Design

by Rob Urbinati

ǁSAMUEL FRENCHǁ

FOR PRODUCTION INQUIRIES

UNITED STATES AND CANADA
info@concordtheatricals.com
1-866-979-0447

UNITED KINGDOM AND EUROPE
licensing@concordtheatricals.co.uk
020-7054-7298

Each title is subject to availability from Concord Theatricals Corp.,
depending upon country of performance. Please be aware that *DEATH
BY DESIGN* may not be licensed by Concord Theatricals Corp. in
your territory. Professional and amateur producers should contact the
nearest Concord Theatricals Corp. office or licensing partner to verify
availability.

MUSIC AND THIRD-PARTY MATERIALS USE NOTE

IMPORTANT BILLING AND CREDIT REQUIREMENTS

DEATH BY DESIGN was originally produced by Houston Family Arts Center, Houston, Texas (Bob Clark, Executive Director; Teri Clark, Artistic Director; Mario Garza, Producing Director) September 9 – 25, 2011 under the direction of Lisa Garza. The Assistant Director was Elaine Edstrom. Set design was by Benjamin Mason, with lighting design by John Baker. The Costume Designer was Linsay Burns, and the Sound Designer was Jonathan Melcher. The Stage Manager was Brendis O'Sullivan. The cast was as follows:

BRIDGIT . . . . .Kathy Drum
JACK . . . . Matt Elliott
EDWARD BENNETT . . . . .Patrick Barton
SOREL BENNETT . . . . Stephanie Morris
WALTER PEARCE . . . . J. Blanchard
ERIC . . . . .Joshua Clark
VICTORIA VAN ROTH . . . . Hannah McKinney
ALICE . . . . Chaney Moore

DEATH BY DESIGN was subsequently produced by Good Theater, Portland, Maine (Brian P. Allen, Executive and Artistic Director; Stephen Underwood, President) January 30 – February 24, 2013 under the direction of Brian P. Allen. Set design was by Craig Robinson, with lighting design by Iain Odlin. The Costume Designer was Justin Cote, and the Sound Designer was Stephen Underwood. The Stage Manager was Michael Lynch. The cast was as follows:

BRIDGIT . . . . .Susan Reilly
JACK . . . . .Benjamin Row
EDWARD BENNETT . . . . Rob Cameron
SOREL BENNETT . . . . Abigail Killeen
WALTER PEARCE . . . . .Paul Haley
ERIC . . . . Matthew Delamater
VICTORIA VAN ROTH . . . . .Janice Gardner
ALICE . . . . Kat Moraros

CHARACTERS

BRIDGIT – the Maid. Irish. Crabby. Warm-hearted. Fifties.

JACK – the Chauffer. Cockney. Charming. Clever. Twenties.

EDWARD BENNETT – the Playwright. Urbane. Vain. Thirties/Forties.

SOREL BENNETT – the Actress. Glamorous. Daffy. Thirties/Forties.

WALTER PEARCE – the Politician. Stiff. Conservative. Thirties/Forties.

ERIC – the Radical. Emphatic. Fiery. Twenties.

VICTORIA VAN ROTH – the Bohemian. Intense. Artistic. Any age.

ALICE – the Visitor. Sweet. Shy. Twenties.

SETTING

The action of the play takes place in the at living room of the Bennett's house at Cookham.

TIME

1932.

AUTHOR'S NOTES

Although *Death by Design* is essentially a comedy, the "murder-mystery" aspects of the play need to be carefully articulated in the production. All of the characters (except Walter, the victim) should be viable suspects, and their behavior should reflect their motives, what they attempt to do to Walter in Act One, and how these evolve over the course of Bridgit's investigation in Act Two. Eric and Bridgit are the only characters who know they are not guilty, and thus, are suspicious of each other and everyone else. Each of the other characters, once they are cleared, also becomes suspicious of the other characters. All of the characters have a motive, however ridiculous, for wanting Walter dead, and these are set up in Act One:

MOTIVES TO KILL WALTER PEARCE:

EDWARD BENNETT – Walter is having an affair with his wife. Also, Edward's career is faltering, so what does he have to lose?

SOREL BENNETT – Walter has insulted her, and proved a disagreeable guest.

VICTORIA VAN ROTH – Jack tells her when he picks her up at the train station that Walter accidentally killed his mother. She's in love with Jack, and a bit unhinged.

ALICE – She knows what Walter did to Jack's mother, and she's aware of JACK's hatred toward WALTER. She wants to do something to win back JACK's affection.

JACK – WALTER accidentally killed his mother, and JACK has been harboring a hatred for him ever since.

ERIC – WALTER stands for everything ERIC is against, politically.

BRIDGIT – WALTER is an annoying guest. And she's been eager to solve a crime.

The actions in the extended "pantomime sequence" near the end of Act One should not be seen by the audience. The area around the sofa, where Walter is "sleeping," should be dark. In this scene, the audience should see who is entering and from where, these characters' actions on the perimeters of the room, and where they exit. But it's useful for the director and actors to know what these characters are doing to Walter during this sequence. Some of this information is discussed in Act Two, but much of it is not.

ACTIONS DURING THE PANTOMIME SEQUENCE
(AND ASSORTED CLUES AND RED HERRINGS):

Edward Bennett pours sleeping draught into the bottle of scotch near the top of Act One, in an effort to put either Walter or Sorel to sleep. He's upset with his wife, knowing that she's planned a rendezvous to annoy him, and the sleeping draught is his attempt to thwart her plan. At the end of Act One, on his way downstairs to check if Walter has drunk the scotch, he sees Eric in the living room, and waits until he leaves. Then, in the pantomime sequence, he approaches Walter, and is not sure if he's dead or asleep (per his discussion about chloral with Bridgit in Act One). In Act Two, when Bridgit proves that Alice missed when she attempted to shoot Walter, Edward assumes that he must be guilty, until Bridgit clears him of this charge. Also, please note that Edward peeks into the room when Jack and Bridgit are talking at the top of Act One, and thus has information about their conversation which he will reveal in Act Two (and use in his play). But he waits to enter, so he can "taint" the scotch.

Annoyed with Walter, Sorel Bennett attempts to make him nauseous by serving him poisonous greens, which she picked to tease Edward into thinking she plans to kill him. In the pantomime sequence, she checks to see if Walter has eaten the salad. (Bridgit has swapped out the poisonous greens, so the salad poses no danger, which Sorel doesn't know) Once Alice is cleared, Sorel thinks she may be guilty, until Bridgit clears her of the charge. On another topic, Sorel knows as soon as Victoria calls from the station that she's come to Cookham to see Jack, but this is their secret.

In the pantomime sequence, Eric comes upstairs to retrieve the Gertrude Lawrence picture book he noticed earlier. He checks to be sure Walter is asleep to save himself from embarrassment, then takes the book and hurries back down to the root cellar. Edward sees this from the stairs, which he will point out in Act Two. Eric has made no attempt on Walter's life, thus, he knows he is not guilty, although he has a secret he wants to keep.

Bridgit enters the room during the pantomime sequence to check on Walter. She checks his pulse and realizes that he is alive and sleeping, and examines his empty glass of scotch, from the bottle she saw Edward taint. She also notices marks around Walter's neck, so she's aware that something more sinister has been perpetrated. After the shot is fired, she reenters the room, and notices the hole in the wall made by the bullet (although this should not be "over-revealed" to the audience). So throughout Act Two, Bridgit knows Walter is alive, but in a deep sleep caused by the sleeping drought. She also recognizes that various attempts have been made on his life, and seeks to discover who perpetrated each of them, for her own amusement. The audience should consider the possibility that Bridigt is the murderer. Also, please note the moment in Act Two where Bridigt cuts the telephone wire with her back to the audience. She does this so she can solve the attempted murder herself, but the audience shouldn't see her cut the wire.

Victoria attempts to strangle Walter with her scarf, and believes she has done so throughout Act Two. When she sees how perceptive BRIDGIT is, she panics and starts to drink. She never learns that her effort has failed, as she passes out drunk.

Alice comes to Cookham to shoot Walter Pearce (with his own gun), in a desperate attempt to win back Jack's affection, which she feels she is losing. She is convinced she is the murderer until Bridgit proves that she missed her target because she wasn't wearing her spectacles, at which point, Alice is suspicious of everyone.

Jack believes that he strangled Walter with his bare hands, killing him. Bridgit knows that Walter is alive, but during Act Two, she (successfully) tries to discover why Alice and Jack would attempt to murder Walter. This is something that Jack never told her.

(Scene: The living room of the country home of Edward and Sorel Bennett. It is very messy. The room is decorated with comfortable furniture including a sofa with pillows, a small end table with a drawer, a few chairs and lamps, and a carpet. The front door is downstage right. French windows are upstage, leading to a garden. A staircase upstage left ascends to the bedrooms, and Edward's study. There is a service door beneath the stairway leading to the kitchen, and to the root cellar. Paintings, a mirror, and a clock adorn the walls. Also in the room are a bookcase, a gramophone, a closet or hat rack, and a bar trolley with liquor, glasses, and an ice bucket.)

*(At rise, **BRIDGIT** is angrily picking up the mess.* **JACK** *enters from the front door in his chauffer's uniform. He has a solid build, and moves with a brisk, cheerful bounce.)*

JACK. *(sneaks up behind her and gives her a hug)* ARGHH!

BRIDGIT. Scared me half to death, Jack! Where've you been?

JACK. Wipin' down the Bentley. It's splashed all over with mud. What ya mutterin' to yerself?

BRIDGIT. The missus ought t' give me fair warnin' when she's comin'! Thinks she can pop in and out anytime she pleases, she does.

JACK. *(Flops down on the sofa and relaxes. With no bitterness:)* 'At's the way the world is designed, luv – the rich in their proper place, tellin' me and you what to do.

BRIDGIT. The larder's empty and there's no time t' go t' the village. I've yet t' buy me Tittle Tattle, even.

9

JACK. They've 'ad another row, they 'ave – a real whopper.

BRIDGIT. Then it won't be long till himself shows up, too. Lager, lad?

JACK. Thank you kindly.

(**BRIDGIT** *exits to the kitchen*. **JACK** *speaks louder so she can hear*.)

The skies opened up when me and Mrs. Bennett was motorin' 'ere. 'Ad to pull over and put up the canopy till it cleared.

(**BRIDGIT** *reenters with a glass of lager*.)

Where's Mrs. B now?

BRIDGIT. In the garden, if you please – assuming the role of lady of the manor. Depend on it, she's up to something this week-end.

JACK. Like clockwork, whenever she gets a poor notice in the Daily Mail –

BRIDGIT. – I best prepare for a performance here in Cookham.

JACK. Newspaper didn't take kindly to Mr. Bennett's writin' neither. Nasty business. So they tussled. *(acts out the fight)* 'E was 'ollerin' like a madman, and she lammed into 'im – whack! – right 'cross the kisser. Then she grabs an Oriental vase and 'urls it at 'is 'ead. Tiny pieces flyin' everywhere.

BRIDGIT. Those vases cost a pretty penny. They should throw pickle jars at each other.

JACK. Then she's out the door, sayin' she quit the show. Never comin' back.

BRIDGIT. That old trick?

JACK. The fight was a good deal livelier than the play.

BRIDGIT. Attendin' the theatre, are ya lad?

JACK. Front row of the stalls. But I got the elbow from the bloke beside me when I started in snorin'. Society women sippin' cocktails make me drowsy.

BRIDGIT. Get enough of that on the job, we do. If I ever attend the theatre –

JACK. Come to town, and I'll ask Mr. B for two tickets.

BRIDGIT. Me mum saw a show once, with a lass fallin' over a cliff. That's something I'd like to see!

JACK. Even before the dust settled, I was readyin' up the Bentley. Damn that downpour. Got me work cut out, alright. She needs to be all shiny when I take 'er for a spin tonight.

BRIDGIT. *(playfully)* And what kind o' sinful thing has yourself got planned?

JACK. This fine evenin' I'll be goin' down to 'Igh Street with a lovely young lass who shall remain nameless.

BRIDGIT. Clara, the redhead.

JACK. I swear, Bridgit – you got the keenest mind in Cook'am.

BRIDGIT. T'ain't nothin'. Last time you come down, I spied a long red hair on ya collar. Here 'tis. *(She opens the drawer and pulls out a long strand of red hair.)* You can do better than her, Jack.

JACK. Randy old 'en – you want me all to yourself.

BRIDGIT. Lookatcha lyin' about. You lack the steam to be keepin' up with the likes of me.

JACK. I'm saltin' it away for tonight.

BRIDGIT. Watch out for these modern women. *(looks around)* Now where's me ball of yarn?

JACK. If I can hide me lady in town from me bird in Cook'am, and keep all of 'em from learnin' about me lass in Kent, I should manage to keep this loaf of bread on me shoulders.

BRIDGIT. Pace yourself, lad. Too many lasses – that's askin' for trouble.

(JACK jumps up, puts his arms around BRIDGIT's waist and lifts her in the air.)

JACK. You're the only one I want.

BRIDGIT. *(squeals and giggles)* Devil! Put me down!

JACK. Squealin' like a lass of sixteen, you are!

(JACK *puts* BRIDGIT *down.*)

BRIDGIT. If you're so keen on liftin' things, why don't you hoist the sofa? Me ball o' yarn must've rolled under.

JACK. 'Ere you go.

(*With no effort,* JACK *lifts and end of the sofa with one arm, revealing a mess beneath.* BRIDGIT *retrieves her yarn.*)

BRIDGIT. A woman up in the air isn't proper, Jack. Someone might see me knickers.

JACK. No one 'ere but you and me, and I seen your knickers plenty.

BRIDGIT. Pokin' through me dresser drawers, are ya?

JACK. Billowin' on the clothesline like sails on a clipper ship.

BRIDGIT. (*lightly*) Don't be bold, Jack. Now get yourself back to work while I make this place fit for the livin'.

JACK. Come sit by me.

BRIDGIT. That's enough foolishness. We don't want Mrs. B seein' the two of us here loafin'.

JACK. She's so scatty she'd walk right by.

(BRIDGIT *returns the strand of hair and pulls a muffler from a drawer in the end table. She sits next to* JACK *as* EDWARD *peeks in the front door, unseen for a few moments, then closes the door.*)

BRIDGIT. I hoped t' finish knittin' the muffler this weekend. Not very likely.

JACK. You're like a mum to me, Bridgit.

BRIDGIT. A good lad, you are. None of these ruffians toolin' round High Street.

JACK. Since the poor dear passed on when I was just a boy, I've never 'ad no one do for me what a mum does.

BRIDGIT. How did she go so young?

JACK. Tis a sorrowful tale.

BRIDGIT. *(noticing he looks sad)* Ay, lad, another time. You without a mum, and me with no kids t' call me own – who else have I got for t' be knittin' a muffler?

JACK. For me, is it?

BRIDGIT. D'ya fancy the color, Jack?

JACK. Matches me eyes.

BRIDGIT. Of course it does. Away on with you, lad! And hop it!

(**JACK** *kisses* **BRIDGIT** *on the cheek, and heads out the front door.* **BRIDGIT** *puts the muffler away and hurries into the kitchen, leaving the door ajar. It's quiet a moment, then* **EDWARD** *opens the front door and enters surreptitiously. He has a bandage on his forehead, and his hair is slicked back. He is carrying newspapers.* **BRIDGIT** *peeks in as he heads to the bar trolley, takes a small vial out of his jacket pocket, and dumps the contents into the bottle of scotch. He hangs his jacket and hat. He sits and opens* The Daily Mail *to the crossword, and takes a pencil out of the drawer. After a few moments,* **BRIDGIT** *enters.)*

EDWARD. Ah, Bridgit. Good afternoon.

BRIDGIT. Welcome, Mr. B.

EDWARD. Your timing is impeccable. What is a five-letter word for "tranquility?" Third letter "a."

BRIDGIT. *(instantly)* Death.

EDWARD. Death, you say. You're in a sour mood.

BRIDGIT. The missus arrives without notice. Now you're here, and there's no tellin' who else'll be turnin' up. I won't have any tranquility till I'm dead and gone. Only in death will I find P – E – A – C – E.

EDWARD. *(writing in the word)* Ah, most kind. Sorry to have upset your schedule, Bridgit. I had an irresistible urge for country air.

BRIDGIT. The country air'd be outside, sir. Had another spat, have ya?

EDWARD. Guilty as charged.

BRIDGIT. Bandage gave it away.

EDWARD. In a normal marriage, one might wonder if I had fallen.

BRIDGIT. If ya don't mind me sayin', t'aint nothin' normal 'bout you and Mrs. B. Use up all your vases that way. Have to put your flowers in soup tins.

EDWARD. Whither the mistress of the manor? Hiding in her boudoir, weeping tears of regret?

BRIDGIT. Prancin' about in the garden, sir.

EDWARD. Wearing one of her preposterous hats, I presume.

BRIDGIT. Looks like a pillow what's losin' its stuffin'.

EDWARD. I'm certain her hat is very fashionable, Bridgit. Sorel Bennett is always *a la mode*.

BRIDGIT. More's the pity. It's big as a tent.

EDWARD. To shield her from the sun's rays. She's obsessed with preserving her youth. Last month, before rehearsals began, she injected monkey glands.

BRIDGIT. You're jokin'!

EDWARD. With Mrs. Bennett, there is never a need to joke. She traffics in self-parody.

BRIDGIT. I told her t' pick some greens for salad. Put her t' work, I did.

EDWARD. A fresh salad before dinner would be superb, Bridgit.

BRIDGIT. Not before dinner, sir – that is dinner. It's all we have – and a tin of sardines.

EDWARD. *(to appease her)* Salad and sardines sounds a poem, Bridgit – an absolute poem.

BRIDGIT. Flattery won't cut any ice with me, sir.

EDWARD. *(suddenly anxious)* I trust the bar trolley is fully stocked?

BRIDGIT. What do I look like – a maid?

EDWARD. *(confused a beat, then)* You do, rather. Have I been suffering under a misconception?

BRIDGIT. *(heads to the bar trolley and picks up the bottle into which he emptied the vial)* I'm not one to grouse, sir, but the furniture needs dustin' and the floors need sweepin' and the silver needs polishin'. And I've yet to read this week's *Tittle Tattle!*

EDWARD. Don't fidget, Bridgit. I promise we will have a peaceful week-end, unless Sorel launches into one of her venomous attacks on my writing, in which case, I shall murder her with an axe.

BRIDGIT. Do it outside. Axes make an awful mess. A fortnight ago, in –

EDWARD. A peace offering. *(hands her a copy of* The Tittle Tattle*)* Picked it up at Maidenhead when I changed trains.

BRIDGIT. Me *Tittle Tattle!* Much obliged, Mr. B. Imagine what kinds of horror might've happened without me knowledge. *(She plops down on the couch, and digs into the paper, flipping the pages.)*

EDWARD. I'm sure the editors would be delighted to learn that your patronage is so – fanatical.

BRIDGIT. Can't miss an issue, sir – what with all these wives and husbands and mistresses and lovers and bits on the side nowadays shootin' and poisonin' and stabbin' and stranglin' each other.

EDWARD. I was unaware that parlors across London were strewn with the bodies of thwarted paramours. The only men and women I've seen on parlor floors are dead drunk.

BRIDGIT. Who said London? All this is happenin' right here in the village.

EDWARD. In Cookham? That must reduce the population considerably.

BRIDGIT. *(with relish)* Just yesterday, a wife done her husband in with a carvin' knife through the back at dinner. Dead as mutton, he was.

EDWARD. Before or after dessert?

BRIDGIT. After, sir.

EDWARD. Well, that shows some courtesy, at least. But it does seem a bit untidy. I'm certain it quite ruined his jacket.

BRIDGIT. And soiled the carpet. These wives don't bother to think when they set to skewerin' their husbands that the carpets'll be bloody all over and the maids have to clean up the mess.

EDWARD. Bridgit, you have my absolute assurance that I shall never attempt to eliminate my wife in any way that would increase your labor.

BRIDGIT. Both Mrs. B and I will be grateful.

EDWARD. And I shall do my utmost to encourage Sorel, whatever homicidal design she may pursue, to keep the carpet foremost in her considerations.

BRIDGIT. Much obliged, sir.

EDWARD. Personally, I feel that poison would be more orderly, and equally effective.

BRIDGIT. Very neat, poison is.

EDWARD. What's the most difficult poison to detect? Your talk of murder has aroused my curiosity.

BRIDGIT. There's aconitine, arsenic, chloral, cyanide, morphine, prussic acid, and strychnine.

EDWARD. *(anxiously)* I believe my sleeping draught contains chloral. Could it prove fatal?

BRIDGIT. One would have to consume an awful lot of it. Most times, it just knocks ya flat for a few hours.

EDWARD. Bridgit, I must say your expertise in these matters is impressive – if a bit unnerving.

BRIDGIT. I could discover whodunit quicker than any of ya posh police – includin' Inspector Benson.

EDWARD. Is that the chap who barged in when Sorel threw herself down the stairs?

BRIDGIT. She claims you gave her a wee push, sir – that's the reason she rang him up.

EDWARD. That was insufficient cause for her to summon the constabulary.

BRIDGIT. Coppers don't know a thing 'bout human nature,

sir. They make up their mind who's the guilty party, and the real evil-doers toddle off easy as ya please. My motto – assume the worst in everyone.

(**JACK** *enters.*)

EDWARD. Your complete lack of faith in human decency is astonishing, Bridgit. I've been sentimentalizing the rustic characters I write.

JACK. *(eagerly)* Put *me* in play, sir!

BRIDGIT. I've been in service longer.

JACK. *(playfully)* Lollin' about, readin' your gory stories. 'Twould tarnish the working class if Mr. B put the likes of you on stage.

EDWARD. I'm afraid I am entirely to blame. I have been assailing Bridgit with inquiries.

BRIDGIT. I'm off. There'll be more time for me *Tittle Tattle* tonight, with a hot toddy!

(*She exits.*)

JACK. Afternoon, Mr. B.

EDWARD. Are you surprised to see me?

JACK. We've trod this path before, sir. *(re: bandage)* Looks like she fetched you a good one.

EDWARD. I wondered why everyone at Paddington Station was staring at me with moist, sympathetic eyes.

JACK. Mrs. B has a mighty arm, I'll give 'er that. If you like, Mr. B, I can teach you 'ow to duck.

EDWARD. That is most kind, Jack. I acquired no practical knowledge whatsover at the Royal Academy of Dramatic Arts. My training in phonetics left me ill-equipped for the perils of married life. I should've taken the seminar in unarmed combat.

JACK. Precisely why I'm a bachelor, Mr. B., and shall remain so all me days.

EDWARD. Jack, what if the right woman happens by?

JACK. The right women 'appen by on a regular basis, Mr. B – in town, 'ere in Cook'am, and back 'ome in Kent.

EDWARD. You should have joined the Navy, and expanded your harem.

JACK. Don't take much to water, sir – it shrinks me willy.

EDWARD. The ideal woman is out there for you somewhere, my boy – unless the popular songs have it entirely wrong.

JACK. Beg pardon, Mr. B, but when I see the way you and Mrs. B carry on, any desire I might 'arbor for wedlock is squashed like a gnat.

EDWARD. Don't be slack, Jack – or you'll end a lonely bachelor.

JACK. Keep the ladies smilin', that's the ticket.

(*JACK exits out the front door, as* **SOREL** *enters through the French windows, grandly. She is wearing an enormous hat with feathers, and carrying a basket of what looks like weeds. She poses as a "country maiden" for* **EDWARD**'s *benefit, but he doesn't turn to look. She places a record on the gramophone – a waltz instrumental, then heads to a mirror on the wall.*)

EDWARD. Sorel, darling, what is an eight letter word for "murder?" Final letter "e."

SOREL. *(instantly)* Marriage.

EDWARD. I believe the editor prefers a synonym – not motivation.

SOREL. I offered a synonym.

EDWARD. Do you intend to murder me? Are you planning a *(as he writes in the word)* hom-i-cide?

SOREL. *(removes the hat)* Time will tell, dear. The week-end has only begun.

EDWARD. It appears a few pigeons have roosted in your bonnet.

SOREL. Is it your intention this afternoon to hurl insults at me like javelins?

EDWARD. Did you choose that lethal metaphor deliberately?

SOREL. Entirely subconscious, darling – but you know what Dr. Freud says.

EDWARD. I was unaware that you were remotely familiar with anything Viennese, apart from the waltz.

SOREL. *(She turns and looks at* **EDWARD** *directly, with deep romantic longing:)* We danced to this tune on the Isle of Capri, do you recall?

EDWARD. Would you be so kind as to have this dance with me now?

SOREL. Oh, darling! *(They dance, blissfully content for a few moments, then:)* I suppose I shan't go anywhere without you pursuing me like a demented hound.

(They space their lines around the music, taking time to dance and dip between.)

EDWARD. Did you think I would remain in our flat amidst a pile of shattered glass?

SOREL. You called me a she-wolf, darling. That was uncharitable.

EDWARD. It was no excuse for you to launch a vase – especially the Ming.

SOREL. You are heartless.

EDWARD. And we are Ming-less. It was spiteful of you, Sorel.

SOREL. The so-called "Ming" belonged to your first wife. It was a cheap imitation, and has been irritating me for years.

EDWARD. You are my first wife, as I have oft reminded you. But very likely not my last.

SOREL. What could I have done to inspire such venom?

EDWARD. Your snoring is particularly oppressive.

SOREL. That bandage is quite dashing.

(The record starts to skip.)

EDWARD. The record is stuck.

SOREL. I believe it's fate, trying to tell us something.

EDWARD. I find fate quite impertinent, actually – always interjecting its views gratuitously, in the vaguest of terms.

(**SOREL** *picks up her basket and sifts through.* **EDWARD** *yanks the needle off the record.*)

SOREL. Our song is ended. The time has come for us to go our several ways.

EDWARD. But we're Siamese Twins. Bosom buddies. Juno's swans. Two peas in a pod –

SOREL. *(interrupting)* You may cling to those tedious idioms when I tell you my news.

EDWARD. Who is it this time?

SOREL. I have invited Walter Pearce for the week-end. You must return to London at once.

EDWARD. You impudent cat. Invite anyone you like – a missionary, or an American for all I care – but I will not permit a politician inside my home.

SOREL. I had not expected you to put in an appearance or I wouldn't have asked him.

EDWARD. You desperately wanted me to follow you here, Sorel – admit it.

SOREL. Can I help if I am irresistible to those in the halls of government?

EDWARD. – where they denounce immorality the week long and totter off to their mistresses come week-end.

SOREL. I am not Walter's mistress, of yet. And he is not a mere politician, darling – he's a diplomatist. I intend to travel the world with him, wearing extravagant hats.

EDWARD. In fact, Mr. Pearce was recently elected, along with many other like-minded charlatans, on a platform dedicated to eliminating decadent behavior entirely.

SOREL. Entirely? That should keep him quite occupied.

EDWARD. They despise people like us, Sorel.

SOREL. Walter Pearce adores me.

EDWARD. *(enraged)* He adores the characters I have written for you – my Daphne, my Beryl, my Ariadne...

SOREL. *(interrupting)* He wants to save me from you!

(**SOREL** *picks up a vase and prepares to hurl it at* **EDWARD***, who raises his fists as* **JACK** *enters. They resume their composure.*)

EDWARD. We mustn't quarrel, Sorel. It will set a bad example for the servants.

JACK. Afternoon, Mrs. B. Done some gardenin'?

SOREL. Yes, Jack, but I am unable to determine which of these greens are edible, and which I might use to poison Mr. Bennett.

JACK. Still at it, eh?

(**BRIDGIT** *enters from the kitchen.*)

BRIDGIT. G'day, Mrs. B. Brung in some provisions, have ya?

SOREL. Bridgit, these greens were at the outer edges of the garden. Do you recognize them?

BRIDGIT. *(peering in the basket)* There's baneberry, black nightingale, foxglove, hemlock, spurges, thornapple and *(suspiciously)* yew.

SOREL. *(apprehensively)* Me?

BRIDGIT. Yew – from the Yew tree. It's poison. They're all poison.

EDWARD. Bridgit, I am flabbergasted. Not only are you able to identify each weed, but once again, you've alphabetized your list.

SOREL. *(overacting)* This is a catastrophe! Whatever will we do for salad?

BRIDGIT. *(pulling out a few leafs of lettuce)* Here's a wee bit of lettuce.

JACK. And there's always a tin of sardines in the larder.

EDWARD. Mr. Pearce will have to find other ways to satisfy his appetites.

JACK. Walter Pearce?

BRIDGIT. What's this?

SOREL. I've asked a friend for the week-end, Bridgit. He should be arriving at the station any moment.

BRIDGIT. Is that so? And what will he be eatin', pray?

SOREL. You'll have to cobble something together with the lettuce and sardines. Not to worry – he's certain to be so utterly mesmerized by my aura he will hardly notice the menu.

EDWARD. He can sleep in the Caligula room.

BRIDGIT. We don't have a Caligula room.

SOREL. We do now, apparently – and I'm certain we've not heard the last of it.

BRIDGIT. There isn't food enough to be gettin' us through the week-end. Mr. Pearce will starve!

SOREL. He will very likely bring chocolates.

EDWARD. Beware, Sorel – your Act Two costume has begun to split at the seams.

JACK. *(dispirited)* Must I take the Bentley back out into the mud?

EDWARD. *(for* **SOREL***'s benefit)* Jack, would you do away with Mr. Pearce on the way back from the station, to spare me the effort?

SOREL. *(for* **EDWARD***'s benefit)* Bridgit, would you be sure to toss some of these greens into Mr. Bennett's dinner salad?

BRIDGIT. *(grabs the basket from* **SOREL***)* What's goin' on here?

JACK. There's a plot afoot, that's for certain.

SOREL. A murder mystery.

EDWARD. I detest those plays. They require the audience to scour every phrase and turn of event for clues.

BRIDGIT. *(threateningly)* We're not expectin' anyone else, are we?

SOREL. This is the entire cast, Bridgit.

JACK. A murder mystery needs a few more suspects, don't it?

BRIDGIT. Not this one!

(She stomps off, with the basket.)

JACK. Off I go, into the muck and mire.

(He exits reluctantly.)

SOREL. *(It's quiet a few moments, then:)* I believe we have offended the servants.

EDWARD. Walter Pearce, of all people. Sorel, how could you?

SOREL. Truth be told, I'm not quite sure whom I've invited. There were throngs of clamoring gentlemen at the first night reception, proffering their cards.

EDWARD. So you shuffled the deck, and summoned whoever was on top?

SOREL. Don't be acid, dear. Must I suffer because the *Daily Mail* detested your latest endeavor?

EDWARD. They didn't care much for your particular brand of caterwauling either.

SOREL. *(enraged)* What am I to do when you've written such a hollow character but to fill her out!?

EDWARD. There is nothing hollow about Daphne, and no need to bellow the entire third act!

SOREL. Daphne is another in an interminable line of world-weary society women, laughing gaily while she nibbles caviar and sips cocktails. Talking of which – fetch me a drink, darling.

*(****EDWARD**** heads to the bar trolley. He considers whether to use the scotch into which he emptied the vial, decides against it, and prepares cocktails for* **SOREL** *and himself. During the above:)*

SOREL. I feel stifled, Edward – asphyxiated. My life is a bore. The same friends, the same cars, the same estates – the same gowns, the same jewels, the same sables – the same dinners, the same cafes, the same parties – the same photographers, the same stylists, the same masseuses – the same injections, the same high-colonics –

EDWARD. *(interrupting)* That's quite enough.

*(***EDWARD*** *hands her a drink.)*

Cheers.

SOREL. All that, I can tolerate. But I beg you, Edward – not the same role.

EDWARD. The women I have written for you are vastly different creations. It's your interpretations that are ploddingly, monotonously the same.

SOREL. I cannot go on this way. I shan't return to the Garrick.

EDWARD. My dear, you will be at the Garrick Monday next when the curtain rises on *Daphne's Delight*, or your youthful and determined understudy will assume the role, which is incidentally more suited to an actress of her range and proportions.

SOREL. All of my most devoted friends insist that I have maintained the figure of a maiden.

EDWARD. A maiden aunt. Face facts, darling. The curtain has closed on our days as Bright Young Things.

SOREL. My public will not stand for an understudy!

EDWARD. If you make this habitual threat once more this week-end, I shall ask Gertrude Lawrence to replace you in the role.

SOREL. *(with disgust)* Gertrude Lawrence is a third-rate hack who has had a tremendous amount of luck.

EDWARD. The *Daily Mail* feels otherwise. "Miss Lawrence confirms beyond doubt that she is the reigning queen of the London stage. She possesses an incandescent charisma that hurls the entire audience into immediate, abject slavery."

SOREL. How dare you memorize that quotation! I am an *artiste*, Edward. I long to perform the great roles!

EDWARD. Which roles, exactly?

SOREL. I'm not entirely sure, but I've heard so much about them. Something classical – or biblical even, where I die in the end.

EDWARD. Need I remind you that your tongue becomes extremely agitated with period dialogue?

SOREL. That is a lie. You saw my Mirabell in the provinces.

EDWARD. It was Millimant and you were horrid. You sounded like a fishmonger.

SOREL. You mean fishwife *(catches herself)* – and I most certainly did not.

EDWARD. You mustn't impugn me for your limitations.

SOREL. And you mustn't subject me to yours. The time has come to extend the parameters of my talents.

EDWARD. Your talents have been stretched to their outer limits, and found wanting. I fully acknowledge that I write similarly shallow entertainments. I console myself with chronic commercial success.

SOREL. Whilst I exist solely to bring truth and beauty to the masses.

EDWARD. Were you possessed of this notion before or after your high colonic?

SOREL. Edward, we must cease this vulgar sparring. This isn't one of your mildly amusing plays – it's our marriage.

EDWARD. – the principal inspiration for any malice in my work.

SOREL. Am I to blame for yearning to consort with a man who is utterly infatuated with me?

EDWARD. I should like to know what his wife thinks of his week-end escapades.

SOREL. Are you certain he has a wife?

EDWARD. Politicians require spouses to be elected. It supports the misconception that they're part of the common herd.

SOREL. *(with satisfaction)* Accordingly, she must be rather plain.

EDWARD. Let us hope she doesn't turn up in Cookham, at any rate. It would send Bridgit round the bend.

SOREL. What chance have I of basking in blind devotion with you sulking about making rude comments?

EDWARD. I promise not to make a single insolent remark if you will permit me to glare malevolently. *(He demonstrates.)*

SOREL. *(amused)* Edward, darling, your ill-manners betray the depth of your affection for me, but they do rather confuse anyone else who is subjected to them.

EDWARD. I had hoped my ill-manners revealed the depth of my loathing for you, and frightened away everyone else.

SOREL. Concede it, dear – you are mad about me. Now do you promise to stay put in your study the entire week-end, as an act of penitence for your multiple grievances?

EDWARD. Am I to be exiled to the tower like Clarence of York?

SOREL. I was unaware we knew anyone at all in York.

EDWARD. Richard III's brother. Murdered at the end of Act One.

SOREL. Let that serve as warning.

(They kiss. The phone rings. BRIDGIT *enters to answer.)*

BRIDGIT. Hallo? Yes, this is the Bennett home. Victoria? *(to the Bennetts)* Someone's at Victoria Station. *(back to phone)* Not Victoria Sta – ? Victoria Van what? Where are ya? Right here in Cookham? Immediately? You'll just have to wait.

(She slams down the phone.)

I don't like this one sliver!

SOREL. *(lightly)* Who was that on the telephone, Bridgit?

BRIDGIT. A Victoria Van Roth. She's at the station, demanding that Jack retrieve her.

SOREL. *(to* EDWARD, *unconvincingly)* What on earth is Victoria doing in Cookham?

EDWARD. You must have invited her.

SOREL. I don't believe I did –

BRIDGIT. Then she can sleep in the attic!

SOREL. – but I was in such a state when I left town I don't quite recall.

BRIDGIT. You two carry on like you own the place.

SOREL. We do, Bridgit. *(a beat, then)* Don't we, Edward?

(The sound of a car arriving, and then car doors closing.)

EDWARD. That's my exit cue. I shall leave you and Mr. Pearce to your gambols, whilst I plot my revenge.

SOREL. While you're up there, be a dear and try to write something worthy of my talents.

(EDWARD climbs the stairs, as SOREL arranges herself in a pose on the sofa. She isn't satisfied, and changes poses, as BRIDGIT watches with disdain. JACK opens the door, and ushers in WALTER PEARCE, who carries a small box of chocolates. He is very stiff.)

JACK. *(solemnly)* Mr. Pearce, at your pleasure.

SOREL. Walter, darling!

WALTER. Sorel, my dearest one! You look rapturous – a perfect painting.

SOREL. Which sort of painting? A Titian, perhaps?

WALTER. *(adoringly)* Like the painting my spinster Aunt Nelly had in her parlor.

SOREL. *(sourly)* Charming. *(releasing herself from her pose)* Do sit down, Walter. You look as if you're about to salute.

(WALTER attempts to hand BRIDGIT his coat and hat. She snarls at him. He backs away and places his coat and hat on a chair.)

BRIDGIT. Bad tidings, Jack. There's a lady at the station needin' a lift.

JACK. What lady?

BRIDGIT. A Miss Van Roth.

JACK. Victoria?

BRIDGIT. – and Mrs. B doesn't even know whether she –

JACK. *(interrupting)* Once more, unto the breach.

(He hurries out the front door.)

WALTER. *(to* **BRIDGIT***)* Bit nippy out there. I'd like a cup of tea, please.

BRIDGIT. Not on your life!

(She exits into the kitchen.)

SOREL. Pay her no mind, dear. She's rather piqued this week-end.

WALTER. Quite impertinent, actually. She should consider herself lucky to be in service nowadays, with so much of the lower class out of work.

SOREL. Bridgit takes an exceedingly dim view of any unheralded modifications in her schedule. Have you brought me a gift, darling?

WALTER. *(He forgot.)* A thousand pardons. *(handing her the box)* For you, dear – chocolates.

*(***SOREL** *takes the box, and demurely nibbles a chocolate.)*

WALTER. Who is Victoria Van Roth, may I ask?

SOREL. She is my dearest friend. Dabbles in all the arts. She's a sculptress, and studies modern dance. I believe she also plays drums in a jazz band. *(pointing to an abstract painting on the wall)* That's a painting of hers, there.

WALTER. I can't make it out. *(squinting)* Is it meant to be a face?

SOREL. It's symbolic.

WALTER. Symbolic of what?

SOREL. I'm not quite sure, actually.

WALTER. Art should convey the plain truth, with none of this modern shilly-shallying. I must convince her. Is Miss Van Roth open to persuasion, or quite set in her ways?

SOREL. Victoria is wide open to all sorts of persuasion – except, perhaps, the sort you have in mind. She's rather bohemian.

WALTER. That won't do at all. There is no time to waste. Difficult days are ahead for this country. We must all buck up!

SOREL. *(flirtatiously)* You are adorably priggish, Walter.

WALTER. I presumed our sojourn would be private.

SOREL. Victoria rather loathes the country. *(unconvincingly)* I haven't the faintest idea why she's come.

WALTER. After a week in the musty halls of government, I find the country air invigorating.

SOREL. I'd have sworn you were a diplomatist.

WALTER. No. I am among hundreds of proud conservatives recently swept into Parliament. The General Election was historic, don't you agree?

SOREL. I was unaware there *was* an election, what with rehearsals and fittings and first night. But you won, darling – how lovely for you!

WALTER. I will put this country back on the right track.

SOREL. *(uninterested)* And not a moment too soon. Now why don't you pour us both a cocktail and sit by me?

WALTER. Brandy?

> *(***WALTER*** *picks up the bottle that* ***EDWARD*** *tampered with, looks at it, then puts it down, picks up another and pours two drinks. During this,* ***SOREL*** *digs into the chocolates ravenously, making rapturous sounds of pleasure. She searches among the wrappers, but having eaten all of them, she tosses the box aside, disappointed.)*

WALTER. I can hardly believe I am alone in a room with the ravishing Sorel Bennett.

SOREL. That's frightfully kind of you, dear. Do go on.

WALTER. What do you mean, go on?

SOREL. I should like very much to wallow in compliments. Use your best butter.

WALTER. The moment when Daphne slammed the door on her husband, then poured herself a cocktail and laughed gaily will be scorched in my memory forever.

SOREL. It is most certainly scorched in *my* memory, given that a variation of it is in every last play that Edward has written for me.

WALTER. *(He hands her the drink, and sits.)* Your Daphne was enchanting, my dear – absolutely enchanting. As was your Beryl, and your Ariadne, and your –

SOREL. *(interrupting, demurely)* What about my Sorel?

WALTER. I have never chanced upon a woman with such extraordinary gifts.

SOREL. Imagine – travelling the world, meeting strangers in far-off lands.

*(**WALTER** tries to interrupt.)*

It would be exhilarating to accompany a diplomatist,

(He tries to interrupt.)

providing no end of occasions to wear exotic hats. What type of hats do you wear when you travel, Walter?

(He tries to interrupt.)

Not pith helmets, I hope – they're rather silly.

WALTER. I beg you to recall that I am a parliamentarian. When I'm not in London, I am at home in Kent.

SOREL. Kent, you say? *(coyly)* Oh, dear. *(moves in closer, and leans against **WALTER**)* You must think me quite daft.

WALTER. *(a beat, then, swooning)* Do I hear soft music playing, or is it your aura?

SOREL. It must certainly be my aura, as Edward has smashed all our gramophone records to bits, apart from one dreary waltz which skips prophetically.

WALTER. You deserve more than an Edward Bennett.

SOREL. Which is precisely why I invited you, brave warrior. Will you protect me from his evil clutches?

WALTER. Delicate flower! You musn't be trampled by his corrupt ways. I shall provide a clear path to guide you.

SOREL. A path whither, darling?

WALTER. The straight and narrow path to righteousness.

SOREL. I am certainly willing to have a go at it – for the week-end, at least.

WALTER. *(knowingly)* You portray women who are jaded with sophistication. A touch of their brittle bearing has stolen into your own behavior. But I see the tender blossom beneath, and I shall unearth it.

SOREL. Walter, I am not certain that you have me entirely right, much as I appreciate the horticultural metaphors.

WALTER. My dear, I know you better than you know yourself.

SOREL. I, too, am able to see deep beneath your stalwart exterior.

WALTER. There is nothing whatever beneath my exterior.

SOREL. That is very likely true. Nevertheless, I perceive the desire under your declarations – the objective disguised by your stated intentions. I am an actress after all. That is my task – and my gift.

WALTER. And here is my gift. *(He kisses her.)*

SOREL. *(loudly, so* **EDWARD** *can hear)* Walter, we musn't! Edward and I are husband and wife. As are you and – what's her name?

WALTER. Don't let's discuss such things. The precious moments we share are few.

SOREL. Fewer than you imagine. *(She cuddles up closer.)* I should like you to whisper something very beautiful to me in my ear.

(He whispers in her ear. She disapproves, angrily.)

Oh, no, that won't do at all!

(He whispers something else.)

Much better.

*(**SOREL** settles her head on his chest. After a few moments, **EDWARD** enters from the top of the stairs in his robe, without the bandage, wearing one of **SOREL**'s hats. **WALTER** jumps up.)*

EDWARD. Press on, old boy. Pay me no mind.

WALTER. We – er – I – er – I was unaware you were in Cookham, Mr. Bennett.

EDWARD. Are you suggesting that you are free to engage in lustful acts with a man's wife in the country, provided her husband is in town?

WALTER. My behavior was not lustful, sir. It was – consoling.

SOREL. I am bitterly disappointed, Walter. I had hoped your intentions were wholly dishonorable.

WALTER. I need a drink.

*(**WALTER** heads to the bar trolley and picks up the brandy.)*

EDWARD. Do try the scotch.

WALTER. We're having brandy.

EDWARD. Damn.

SOREL. Edward, remove that ridiculous hat. It's not at all becoming on you.

EDWARD. Then you agree that it is ridiculous?

SOREL. Walter is quite certain that you are depraved. You needn't make an entrance done up as a country maiden to convince him.

*(**EDWARD** descends the staircase grandly, still wearing the hat.)*

EDWARD. Sorel, who is this man, this "Walter" who has barged into our home?

WALTER. *(***WALTER** *approaches, and shakes* **EDWARD***'s hand.)* Walter Pearce. Parliamentarian.

EDWARD. Edward Bennett. Platitudinarian.

WALTER. We met briefly at your first night reception.

EDWARD. Were you among that obsequious claque suffocating my wife?

WALTER. I offered Mrs. Bennett my card, and she kindly invited me to Cookham for the week-end.

EDWARD. Very cheeky of you, Sorel, I must say – knowing I would be here.

SOREL. I most certainly did not!

EDWARD. *(to* **WALTER***)* Sorel insists that she did not request your presence, sir. To show up without invitation is boorish and ill-mannered.

SOREL. Don't be tiresome, Edward. I am almost certain I summoned Mr. Pearce for the week-end.

WALTER. Almost?

SOREL. You don't look at all like the man I thought I had sent for – the diplomatist.

WALTER. But I gave you my card.

EDWARD. Every man who meets the modestly talented Sorel Bennett offers his card. Our bedroom in town is strewn with them. It looks as if a ticker-tape parade has passed through. One would think she had swum the English Channel.

SOREL. Perhaps I may.

EDWARD. Soon, I hope.

SOREL. Do shut up, Edward. And if you wouldn't mind, Walter and I wish to resume our tete-a-tete.

EDWARD. I shall attend to the garden, whilst you and Caligula here –

WALTER. *(interrupting)* Now just a minute, sir.

EDWARD. You needn't falter, Walter. Your secrets are safe with me.

WALTER. Secrets?

EDWARD. That I discovered my wife locked in your embrace mustn't persuade you that I would use this information to interfere in any way with your vaulting political ambitions. Ta-ta.

(He exits through the French doors to the garden.)

SOREL. Edward is beastly when he becomes jealous. I'm quite certain that's why his first wife left him. He wounds me deeply. Comfort me, kind sir.

WALTER. Perhaps we might take a stroll to Maidenhead.

SOREL. *(assuming a helpless pose)* Walter, can't you see that I am prostrate with grief.

WALTER. I suppose there's no harm – *(sits next to her)* Sorel, my dear – you deserve much more than that popinjay could ever hope to supply.

SOREL. *(moves in closer)* Tell me, Walter, in what ways am I extraordinary?

*(***BRIDGIT*** *opens the kitchen door, peering out at* ***WALTER*** *and* ***SOREL***. *She growls audibly.* ***WALTER*** *pushes* ***SOREL*** *away.* ***BRIDGIT*** *returns into the kitchen with a harrumph.)*

WALTER. What an appalling creature!

SOREL. Rest assured that she treats Edward and me with equal disdain.

WALTER. Why ever do you keep her on?

SOREL. We can only keep on very bad maids. Good maids won't have us.

*(***SOREL*** *and* ***WALTER*** *settle comfortably again for a moment, then the front door bursts open and* ***ERIC***, *disheveled and sweaty, charges in.)*

ERIC. *(breathlessly)* Where is Edward Bennett?

SOREL. Gardening.

*(***ERIC*** *dashes out of the French doors.)*

WALTER. Who on earth was that?

SOREL. Pay him no mind. You were about to enumerate my charms. Now be quick about it. *(She tries to reinsinuate herself into* **WALTER***'s arms.)*

*(***EDWARD*** dashes in through the French windows, holding the hat. He heads to the bar and pours a drink.* **ERIC** *barges in.* **WALTER***, frightened, separates from* **SOREL***, who is amused.)*

ERIC. Mr. Bennett – I've found you at last!

EDWARD. How did you know I was in Cookham?

ERIC. Your flat in London was empty.

EDWARD. You've been prohibited from entering our flat.

ERIC. I crawled up the drainpipe and peered through the window. No one was inside – just a pile of rubble, so I bicycled here.

WALTER. From London? That's thirty-five miles!

SOREL. You must have very muscular thighs.

ERIC. There is no time to waste! Conservatives have taken control of Parliament. We are all doomed!

WALTER. Rubbish. *(to* **SOREL***)* Who is this lunatic?

SOREL. *(to* **WALTER***)* Careful. Eric is perpetually feverish. You mustn't inflame him further or he might explode.

WALTER. Now is the perfect time for us to take a stroll to Maidenhead.

EDWARD. That would be an exceedingly long stroll for you, Sorel.

ERIC. Cease this bourgeois prattle!

EDWARD. I found that remark quite amusing, actually. I shall put it in my next play.

SOREL. Eric, I thought you had been institutionalized.

ERIC. I just escaped.

SOREL. *(impressed)* How very clever.

ERIC. Mr. Bennett, you are a celebrated writer –

SOREL. But not a very good one, actually.

ERIC. The world adores you –

SOREL. For an opposing view, I refer you to today's *Daily Mail.*

ERIC. The time has come for you to put your influence to the greater good. You must forsake cocktails and caviar, and write plays which inspire the working class.

SOREL. Don't be silly, Eric. Those people can't afford to go to the theatre.

EDWARD. Why is everyone dead set against cocktails and caviar of late? I've been quite partial to them since the day I was weaned.

ERIC. I bemoan the waste you have made of your skills.

SOREL. If I am forced to attend a play with a message, I shan't dress.

(**BRIDGIT** *enters from the kitchen.*)

BRIDGIT. What's all this hollerin'? *(re:* **ERIC***)* Who's this mangy mutt?

ERIC. *(to* **EDWARD***, re:* **BRIDGIT***)* You flaunt your wealth, whilst workers such as she can barely scrape by.

EDWARD. I must keep Sorel in hats.

SOREL. Thank you, darling.

ERIC. *(to* **EDWARD***)* Face facts, Mr. Bennett. Your days as a Bright Young Thing are over.

EDWARD. *(stung)* I should like a cocktail. *(He heads for the bar trolley.)*

ERIC. There is no time for drink!

SOREL. *(casually)* Surely you must make time, Eric, or you will dehydrate.

ERIC. I shall not imbibe while one person is thirsty – nor shall I consume while one person is hungry.

BRIDGIT. How long will you be stayin', lad?

ERIC. Till I persuade Mr. Bennett to see the evil of his ways!

EDWARD. Don't behave like an hysteric, Eric.

BRIDGIT. If you're spendin' the night, you'll have to sleep in the root cellar. *(indicating the kitchen)* It's through here.

ERIC. There is no time for sleep! The world is on the brink of collapse – *(to* **EDWARD***)* but you hold the key to its survival.

WALTER. Young man, let me assure you that the planet's endurance hardly depends upon the likes of Edward Bennett.

ERIC. *(to* **WALTER***)* Hold on – you're Walter Pearce! You're the worst of the lot! You and your ilk will drag this country into the sewer!

WALTER. The country is already in the sewer. My – ilk and I shall exhume it.

EDWARD. And your first initiative is to seduce my wife?

SOREL. Am I part of a political agenda? How delicious!

ERIC. Mr. Bennett, let's away to your study, and toil together. *(He puts a foot on the chair, and poses valiantly.)* With my vision and your talent, we shall create a work that will enrich all mankind!

BRIDGIT. Off the furniture, laddie.

SOREL. Eric, mightn't you tidy up after all that pedaling?

ERIC. There is no time for tidiness!

EDWARD. *(to* **SOREL***)* You should have seen that coming.

ERIC. "Who is the greater sinner – he who robs a bank, or he who owns a bank?"

EDWARD. He who poses the question.

WALTER. You wish to do away with the free enterprise system?

ERIC. Profit and wealth must be distributed equally.

SOREL. Eric, if you insist, I shall offer some of my hats to charity.

ERIC. The poor do not want your hats!

EDWARD. Their lives are sufficiently challenging without exposing themselves to ridicule.

SOREL. *(wounded)* There has been entirely too much abuse directed at my millinery this week-end. I find it quite insensitive, actually. From this day forward, I shall wear only muslin mob-caps with a lace ruffle round the face and neck. I trust that will appease everyone.

ERIC. You have missed my meaning entirely!

SOREL. Eric, I am thoroughly confused. Come sit by me and explain. Now try not to shout, and we shall get along like a house on fire.

(ERIC sits on the sofa. SOREL is between the two men.)

SOREL. *(taking ERIC's hand in hers)* What lovely hands you have. I trust you play the piano?

ERIC. A useless occupation. I have vowed to engage exclusively in pursuits that can rouse the masses.

EDWARD. The bugle, perhaps?

BRIDGIT. Leave the masses be. They deserve a rest.

WALTER. I am fed to the teeth with this discussion. *(He heads for the bar trolley.)*

SOREL. Walter, you must allow that I have many admirers, Eric among them. Isn't that so, Eric?

ERIC. You are a great artist, Mrs. Bennett.

SOREL. Exactly what type of plays do you propose Mr. Bennett writes, mindful that his talents are extremely meager?

ERIC. Plays of social significance – like those of my idol, Bertol Brecht.

WALTER. Sounds like a Kraut.

EDWARD. Don't let's be beastly to the Germans, Walter.

SOREL. After all, we won the war. *(a beat, then:)* Didn't we, Edward?

WALTER. I fought on the front lines!

ERIC. *(cynically)* Bully for you.

WALTER. *(to ERIC)* Are you mad?

SOREL. Yes he is, Walter. His wits went woolgathering years ago. Now do be quiet, or I shall send you home.

EDWARD. *(to WALTER)* Play along, old boy.

*(**WALTER** returns to the sofa. **SOREL** is again between the two men.)*

SOREL. *(to **ERIC**, eagerly)* Tell me, Eric – is there a leading woman's role in this type of play, or just an ensemble of workers waving fists and banners?

ERIC. His *St. Joan of the Stockyards* features a great female lead.

SOREL. *(intrigued)* Joan of Arc?

ERIC. Brecht modernized the historical figure to emphasize the worker's plight. You would be outstanding in the part, Mrs. Bennett.

SOREL. Your timing is serendipitous, Eric. Joan of Arc is precisely the type of heroine I've longed to portray. And in the end, she is burned at the stake. What a finale!

EDWARD. Are you certain your limited abilities would penetrate a suit of armor?

SOREL. Hush, Edward. *(to **ERIC**, eagerly)* What type of hats does she wear?

WALTER. I believe Joan of Arc wore a helmet.

SOREL. Oh, that won't do at all!

ERIC. She works in a meat-packing plant. I doubt she would wear anything elaborate as it might be caught in the machinery.

SOREL. Eric, I feel that somehow, this meat-packing Joan of Arc is not suited to my particular gifts.

EDWARD. And I wished so to see you go up in flames.

SOREL. You couldn't care less about my career. You are cruel, Edward, cruel and heartless! Soothe me, Eric.

*(She flings herself into **ERIC**'s arms, and puts her legs up on **WALTER**.)*

*(**JACK** opens the front door, as **BRIDGIT** enters from the kitchen.)*

JACK. Miss Victoria Van Roth is arrived from London.

(**VICTORIA** *doesn't enter.* **JACK** *peeks outside. He whistles, with two fingers in his mouth.* **VICTORIA** *makes a grand entrance, wearing a sleeveless sarong, one large earring and an extremely long scarf. She stops and poses.*)

VICTORIA. Sorel, darling!

(**SOREL** *rushes to* **VICTORIA,** *and they kiss on both cheeks.*)

SOREL. Victoria! What an agreeable surprise! I understood you were performing this week-end.

VICTORIA. I abandoned my recital at the Van Laban Dance Studio mid-step so that I might hasten to Cookham to console you.

(**VICTORIA** *rushes to* **EDWARD,** *and* **SOREL** *returns to the sofa.*)

Edward, you are a beast. How dare you torment this queen?

EDWARD. *(indicates* **SOREL** *sitting between the two men)* She seems to have recovered admirably.

VICTORIA. Merely a façade to disguise her pain. Sorel, you must see one of my psychoanalysts.

ERIC. You have more than one psychoanalyst? That is bourgeois indulgence.

VICTORIA. I have two, who offer contrasting diagnoses of my mental condition.

SOREL. I should very much like to meet both of these psychoanalysts to learn which one offers guidance that corresponds most directly to my intentions.

EDWARD. Rest easy, Victoria. Sorel is in the firm, manly hands of Mr. Walter Pearce, staunch defender of morality.

VICTORIA. *(glaring suspiciously at* **ERIC** *and* **WALTER***)* Which one of you is Walter Pearce?

(Hesitatingly, **WALTER** *raises his hand.)*

VICTORIA. Morality is hypocrisy in a Sunday suit. I will not allow any such posture to encumber the journey I am taking into the recesses of my psyche.

EDWARD. Bon voyage.

WALTER. England needs you to put your nose to the grindstone, Miss Van Roth.

VICTORIA. What is this "grindstone?" In my dance – nay, in all my artistic pursuits – I use every sinew and corpuscle to receive and to communicate – which includes my nose!

(She breaths in and out heavily, flaring her nostrils wildly.)

JACK. I once knew a bloke who could lick his own elbow.

SOREL. *(just noticing)* Victoria, you seem to have lost an earring.

VICTORIA. I have not. *(indicating her blue stone earring)* I wear one Lapis Lazuli. And I shave only one underarm.

*(**VICTORIA** puts her hands behind her head. One underarm is shaved clean, and there is shock of hair in the other.)*

SOREL. I must say, that's quite *outré*.

WALTER. It's disgusting.

EDWARD. At ease, Victoria.

*(**VICTORIA** puts her arms down.)*

ERIC. Who is this Van Laban?

VICTORIA. Rudolph is a god. His dance techniques demand penetrating personal exploration.

EDWARD. Victoria, it is exceedingly kind of you to take time out from your penetrating personal explorations to minister to my wife.

BRIDGIT. You'll have to sleep in the attic, Miss. I'll air the room out.

VICTORIA. Keep the foul and pestilent vapors out of doors where they belong!

BRIDGIT. Nothin' foul down here unless you brought it.

VICTORIA. All country villages are stagnant pools. To

reside in one is not living – it is loitering.

ERIC. You prefer the congested fumes of London's industries?

VICTORIA. They invigorate me!

WALTER. Exactly what type of dance do you do, Miss Van Roth?

VICTORIA. I shall demonstrate. *(to* EDWARD*)* You – ogre – when I say "commence" beat the table thus. *(She demonstrates, beating the table with her hand.)*

(indicating SOREL*)* Beating is clearly within your area of expertise. *(to* ERIC*)* And you, tousled youth – rattle the ice bucket thus. *(She demonstrates.)* I will create an improvised work, using the latest modern dance techniques. It shall be called – "Wall."

EDWARD. Walter, would you care to participate?

WALTER. I prefer to sit on the sidelines and watch.

VICTORIA. *(to* WALTER, *firmly)* Stand, man.

WALTER. Now, just a minute.

VICTORIA. I said stand!

*(*VICTORIA *reveals her unshaven armpit.* WALTER, *frightened, jumps up and obeys.* VICTORIA *indicates a place for him to stand.)*

VICTORIA. You represent Wall.

SOREL. You have the title role, Walter. That's very good.

WALTER. Do you mean that I'm – a partition?

VICTORIA. You are a barrier – an obstruction.

SOREL. Victoria, what part am I to play?

VICTORIA. *(improvising)* You shall be Tree, casting a shadow over Wall.

SOREL. *(intrigued)* What sort of Tree? A Royal Empress, perhaps?

EDWARD. A Dogwood, with age rings.

VICTORIA. Tree will respond intuitively to the inner meaning of the piece through the movement of her branches.

SOREL. I embrace the challenge!

VICTORIA. Art is nigh! Let us commence!

(**EDWARD** *bangs the table and* **ERIC** *shakes the ice bucket, providing a rhythmic accompaniment to* **VICTORIA**'s *dance.* **SOREL** *stands and assumes the role of Tree, with her arms spread like limbs.* **JACK** *and* **BRIDGIT** *watch, perplexed.* **VICTORIA** *moves about the room slowly, in sweeping, Martha Graham-like moves, stopping with exaggerated poses every now and then near* **WALTER**, *"struggling" to suggest through dance that she cannot get around him. She is intensely serious, and occasionally rearranges her scarf with her arms, creating web-like shapes.* **WALTER** *remains stiff and wall-like. He is annoyed, but doesn't want to disappoint* **SOREL**. **EDWARD** *is amused by* **WALTER**'s *discomfort.* **SOREL**, *as Tree, adjusts her limbs as she tries to interpret* **VICTORIA**'s *intentions.* **BRIDGIT** *and* **JACK** *remain perplexed. In one of her moves,* **VICTORIA** *nearly swipes* **BRIDGIT**'s *head with her arm, but* **BRIDGIT** *ducks just in time.* **VICTORIA** *approaches* **WALTER** *and in one quick move, completely smothers his head in her scarf.*)

WALTER. (*struggling to escape from the scarf*) Let me out!

(**ERIC** *and* **EDWARD** *cease their accompaniment.* **SOREL** *applauds wildly.* **WALTER** *disentangles himself, as:*)

VICTORIA. In Part Two, I shall trample Wall beneath my feet.

SOREL. And Tree will bury him in leaves.

EDWARD. What say you, Walter?

WALTER. Part Two!? Rot!

EDWARD. Wall must be recast.

ERIC. I haven't the slightest idea what any of that was meant to signify.

VICTORIA. There is no single "meaning." Endow the piece with your own interpretation.

ERIC. But if it's incomprehensible, what's the point?

WALTER. It pains me to agree with this fanatical youth, but he is spot on.

SOREL. Ignore them, Victoria. The piece was marvelous.

WALTER. I cannot tolerate another minute in this house. You are all raving mad!

JACK. 'Appy to give you a lift to the station, guv'ner.

SOREL. Walter, you are in the presence of genius.

WALTER. I was unaware when I accepted your invitation this week-end that I would be center-ring in a circus!

ERIC. I found the performance deeply flawed.

VICTORIA. *(with deep contralto resentment)* Flawed? In what way, "flawed?"

ERIC. The piece was too abstract to be of any real significance. And to be frank, plumb silly.

VICTORIA. Hooligan! Jackal!

ERIC. Oh, my. I have aroused the wrath of Victoria Van Roth.

EDWARD. I say, Eric, you're becoming quite catty.

ERIC. I learned from the Master, Mr. Bennett.

VICTORIA. Sorel, I did not hurl myself into this fetid country air to be subjected to these heretics you call friends.

SOREL. Victoria darling, Eric is not my friend. He is in hot pursuit of Edward.

VICTORIA. Interesting.

SOREL. As for Mr. Pearce, he is not at all whom I meant to invite.

WALTER. Truth be told, I have been attending Gertrude Lawrence's first night receptions for years, leaving my cards. It was only because she has never extended an invitation that I accepted yours.

SOREL. Gertrude Lawrence? Is that so?

*(**SOREL**, in one quick move, picks up a pillow from*

the sofa and slams **WALTER** *in the face.)*

JACK. Good one, Mrs. B!

WALTER. This is appalling. It is exactly what would come from government funding of the arts!

(A unison gasp from **EDWARD, SOREL, VICTORIA** *and* **ERIC***. Then* **VICTORIA** *rushes to* **WALTER** *and wraps her scarf around his neck, trying to strangle him.* **WALTER** *struggles to protect himself, and ends up with the scarf adorning his neck.)*

EDWARD. That looks lovely on you. Here, try this.

(He puts **SOREL***'s gardening hat on* **WALTER***.)*

WALTER. I will see to it that not one penny is given to bohemians and fanatics and radicals or any other crackpots who call themselves artists!

(He flings the hat and scarf to the floor.)

You are all moral degenerates!

*(***WALTER** *heads for the door.)*

BRIDGIT. The last train left hours ago.

VICTORIA. Sorel, I must flee this philistine-infested room at once.

EDWARD. You can sleep in the Lucrezia Borgia room.

SOREL. Enough, Edward. Victoria, repair to my bedroom, whilst I prepare the lettuce for Mr. Pearce.

VICTORIA. *(to* **WALTER***)* Wall, your days are numbered.

*(***VICTORIA** *makes a dramatic exit up the stairs, as* **SOREL** *heads into the kitchen.)*

EDWARD. My percussive endeavors have quite worn me out. Presently, I shall take a long, luxurious bath in capitalist bubbles. *(to* **WALTER** *and* **ERIC***)* When I return, I presume that only one of you two gentlemen will be alive. *(looks at* **BRIDGIT***)* Whatever you do, please do not stain the carpet.

BRIDGIT. Much obliged, Mr. B.

*(***EDWARD** *exits up the stairs.)*

WALTER. *(to BRIDGIT)* Might I have a spot of tea?

BRIDGIT. You'll be gettin' lettuce, and I don't want to hear another peep out of ya. I shall prepare the Caligula room.

(She exits up the stairs.)

WALTER. *(to himself, mostly)* That is the most insolent maid I have ever encountered.

JACK. A bit testy this week-end, sir. Matter of fact, we all are.

WALTER. If she were in my employ, I would dismiss her on the spot.

JACK. She's too decent to be workin' for the likes of Walter Pearce.

WALTER. How dare you speak to me in that manner?

JACK. G'night, sir. 'Ave a nice, long rest. *(exits out the front door)*

WALTER. Only a couple as deranged as the Bennetts would keep those two on staff.

ERIC. You expect courtesy from the workers who slave for you?

WALTER. I demand it.

ERIC. It's high time your entire class was exterminated!

(ERIC heads for the bookshelves, looking at the "spines." He lingers for a moment over a large "coffee table" book, but doesn't remove it from the shelf. SOREL enters carrying a tray which holds cutlery, a napkin, and a small plate with one leaf of lettuce. She plops it down on the end table.)

SOREL. Adieu, Walter. I regret that it had to end this way.

(She exits up the stairs.)

(WALTER heads to the bar trolley. He pours himself a drink from the bottle of scotch and sits. ERIC picks up the knife on WALTER's tray and toys with it, staring at WALTER.)

WALTER. Let me rest in peace!

ERIC. I will do precisely that.

(**ERIC** *puts the knife in his inner jacket pocket.* **WALTER** *arranges the tray on his lap and devours the salad.* **ERIC** *watches him eat for a moment, then shuts off one of the lamps and exits through the kitchen.* **WALTER** *finishes eating, puts the tray on the end table, shuts off the other lamp, lies on the sofa, and sighs heavily. It is dark. A clock ticks as time passes. Moonlight spills into the room, but none of it reaches the sofa, where* **WALTER** *begins to snore lightly. Lights shift. The clock ticks loudly throughout the "pantomime" sequence below. Other sound effects such as creaking stairs and doors can be added as characters enter and exit. The area around the sofa is dark, and it is not possible to see any activities that take place there. Visibility is slightly better in other areas of the room.)*

(**EDWARD** *appears on the stairway. He stops as* **ERIC** *opens the kitchen door slowly, enters the room, then moves to the sofa and does something we can't see.* **ERIC** *brandishes his knife, crosses to the bookshelf, does something with his back to the audience, then exits through the kitchen.)*

(*Once* **ERIC** *exits,* **EDWARD** *descends the stairs, crosses to the bar trolley, and examines the bottle of scotch. He crosses to the sofa, does something we can't see, and heads back upstairs.)*

(**JACK** *enters from the front door, flexes his fingers, crosses behind the sofa, and does something we can't see.* **VICTORIA** *appears on the stairs, still wearing her scarf. She peeks into the living room.* **JACK** *sees her and hurries out the front door.)*

(**VICTORIA** *crosses behind the sofa and does something we can't see.* **SOREL** *appears at the top of the stairs.* **VICTORIA** *sees her and hurries out the front door.* **SOREL** *poses momentarily in the* *mirror, crosses to the sofa, does something we can't see, then heads back upstairs.* **BRIDGIT** *enters, pokes around a bit, approaches* **WALTER***, does something we can't see, and exits into the garden.)*

(A woman enters through the front door. She puts her large handbag down and approaches the sofa. She does something we can't see. After a moment, she shoots. Sound: a loud shot. All at once, everyone rushes into the room and hovers near the doorway from which they exited.)

BRIDGIT. Everyone stay right where you are!

*(***BRIDGIT*** enters through the French Windows and turns on a lamp. We see:* **SOREL** *and* **EDWARD** *on the stairway,* **JACK** *and* **VICTORIA***, without her scarf, at the front door, and* **ERIC** *at the kitchen door.* **WALTER***'s arms are akimbo, and he looks quite dead. Also present is* **ALICE***, a plain, gentle-looking young woman holding a pistol with both hands.)*

EDWARD. She shot him!

BRIDGIT. Not so fast.

SOREL. Is that his wife – what's her name?

ALICE. Alice.

EDWARD. Alice Pearce?

BRIDGIT. Batten down the hatches, laddies!

(Simultaneously, **JACK** *closes the front door and* **ERIC** *closes the service door.)*

No one leaves this room till I discover who murdered Walter Pearce!

(The curtain crashes down.)

END OF ACT ONE

ACT TWO

(The living room of the country home of Edward and Sorel Bennett. Everyone is exactly where they were at the end of Act One.)

EDWARD. What was that again?

BRIDGIT. I said no one leaves this room till I discover who murdered Walter Pearce.

EDWARD. But we know exactly who did it.

BRIDGIT. Is that so? And how do we know, pray?

SOREL. A woman is standing just there, brandishing a pistol.

VICTORIA. And it's pointed directly at the victim.

ERIC. One could hardly call that brandishing – her hands are trembling.

SOREL. Eric, I will not allow criticism of my verbs.

EDWARD. Word choice to one side, I prefer that she set the pistol down.

ALICE. I shall return it to my purse. Wherever have I put it?

(Alice, still aiming the pistol, turns in a sweeping move, and each person in the cast ducks as the pistol points at them.)

JACK. *(kindly)* Might I 'ave the weapon, Alice?

ALICE. I'd like to keep it as a memento.

ERIC. *(Locates a large, heavy traveling bag, and struggling, he hands it to* **ALICE**.*)* You are clearly overburdened with material possessions.

SOREL. Though not overburdened with taste, I'm afraid. That's hardly what one would call a purse, Alice – more a trunk with straps.

JACK. What are you luggin' about?

EDWARD. Perhaps the manuscript of a novel or an infant child – but that's another play entirely.

ERIC. Not more artillery, I hope.

ALICE. *(holding up the gun)* I have only the one pistol.

BRIDGIT. Where did you acquire it, lass?

ALICE. It belonged to Mr. Pearce.

> (ALICE *feels her way to the sofa, but misses when she tries to sit, and falls to the floor. The pistol fires accidentally, and Victoria's painting crashes to the ground.)*

VICTORIA. That fiend has shot my painting!

ERIC. She should be rewarded.

VICTORIA. Art has been assassinated. Woe, woe!

> (VICTORIA *picks up the painting and clutches it to her.* JACK *helps* ALICE *up and guides her to the sofa.* BRIDGIT *crosses to the telephone and does something with her back to the audience.)*

SOREL. *(casually)* Victoria, darling, exactly what did that painting represent? The recently deceased and I were musing over it earlier *(wistfully)* – and now, he shall never know.

EDWARD. *(tough luck)* Hard cheese.

VICTORIA. The idea appeared to me as if in a vision –

ERIC. *(interrupting)* This is hardly the time to elucidate your obscure artistic endeavors, Miss Von Wrath.

VICTORIA. *(to* ERIC*) Van Roth!* Listen, boy, there is one dead man in the room already –

EDWARD. – and one dead painting.

VICTORIA. Nothing would please me more than to increase the body count.

ERIC. This is hardly the time to gratify any –

VICTORIA. *(interrupting)* If you say "this is hardly the time" one more time, it will be the last time.

BRIDGIT. Let's have no more talk of killin'. Got me hands

full with the one.

VICTORIA. That boy is deeply aggravating.

EDWARD. Political convictions invariably bring out the worst in people, which is why I am staunchly apolitical, and shall remain so all my days.

SOREL. Nonetheless, the worst in you somehow manages to surface.

(**ALICE***, seated next to* **SOREL***, places the pistol in her purse and cries again, a bit louder.*)

EDWARD. Alice, please do not whimper. It annoys me.

SOREL. *(to* **ALICE***)* Moreover, dear, having spent time in the company of Walter Pearce, everyone in this room would agree that you had ample cause for murder.

JACK. Nothin' to be done about it now.

BRIDGIT. The obvious suspect is never guilty.

ALICE. I shot him, I confess.

BRIDGIT. That cat won't fly, dearie.

EDWARD. But she was caught red-handed.

SOREL. What difference does it make who killed Walter? He's dead and gone. We mustn't let it ruin our week-end. What say we play a parlor game?

EDWARD. That suggestion wants tact, dear – even for my taste.

SOREL. Perhaps we could restore Walter to life.

ALICE. Oh no! *(She cries.)*

EDWARD. *(becoming annoyed)* Rein it in, Alice.

SOREL. Shall I ring up a clairvoyant to conduct a séance? She'd have him back on his feet in no time.

EDWARD. "What is done cannot be undone."

SOREL. What's that from, darling?

EDWARD. The Scottish play.

SOREL. What Scottish play? Surely there's more than one.

ERIC. *(approaches* **WALTER** *cautiously)* Are we certain Mr. Pearce is dead?

EDWARD. I have seen countless actors play dead in that exact position – arms splayed, jaw agape. I am entirely convinced that Walter has shuffled off this mortal coil.

ERIC. The techniques involved with simulating death onstage must not replace medical diagnosis!

BRIDGIT. Simmer down, lad.

SOREL. Perhaps Walter is a very good actor, pretending to be dead out of spite.

EDWARD. His interpretation of Wall was entirely convincing.

SOREL. He was type-cast.

VICTORIA. And only marginally more stiff at present than when he was alive.

ALICE. As the guilty party, I am eager for confirmation that the victim is, in fact, deceased.

ERIC. I shall ring up a Doctor *(He picks up the telephone.)* Hello? Hello? There's no operator.

BRIDGIT. *(holding up the cut wire)* The telephone wire has been severed!

ALICE. Oh, no!

(Everyone looks at everyone else suspiciously.)

ERIC. We should take him to hospital at once.

BRIDGIT. Ever been to the infirmary in Cookham, lad? You enter with a splinter in your finger, and walk out with one arm.

ERIC. I'll bicycle to the Police Station and notify an Inspector.

JACK. We won't be needin' any coppers, right Bridgit?

BRIDGIT. I will solve the murder meself, I will – usin' just me intuition. Now try and stop me!

EDWARD. Thus concludes discussion on the topic.

SOREL. Bridgit, when you stipulate that no one leaves the room, does that include the deceased? I don't fancy sharing the sofa with a cadaver.

BRIDGIT. Mustn't be tamperin' with the evidence, m'am.

ERIC. Mrs. Bennett, I must say I find your comments

extremely callous. A man is dead.

EDWARD. We may console ourselves with the knowledge that there will be one less voice against Government funding of the arts.

VICTORIA. He deserved to die for that alone.

BRIDGIT. Are ya sayin' ya killed him, Miss?

VICTORIA. A lot of people deserve to die. *(indicating* **ERIC***)* That one, for example, is ripe for extinction.

BRIDGIT. Each and every one of you had a reason for wantin' Walter Pearce dead.

SOREL. I certainly did. He was extremely tiresome.

ERIC. The old guard must fall.

JACK. Won't be missed, that's for sure.

VICTORIA. I am indebted to whoever is responsible.

EDWARD. I take your point, Bridgit. There is a chilling lack of sympathy in this room.

ALICE. But wanting someone dead and actually killing them are two very different matters.

BRIDGIT. Two different matters for all but one a ya!

SOREL. It would be deceitful of me to say I am pained even slightly by having a disagreeable guest conveniently eliminated.

BRIDGIT. Meanin' you're the killer, Mrs. B?

SOREL. Surely there are more suitable ways to rid oneself of irritating guests than to murder them.

EDWARD. It is never easy, darling, as you well know. I had some success recently, after a reception. I played a gramophone record quite loud – it was Ethel Merman, singing "I Got Rhythm." The guests fled as if the room were ablaze.

VICTORIA. Murder is quicker.

EDWARD. But Miss Merman is within the parameters of the law – inexplicably.

SOREL. I begged Walter to leave, but apparently, my radiance rendered him immobile.

ALICE. It is truly an honor to meet you, Mrs. Bennett.

SOREL. *(sincerely)* I imagine it must be.

ALICE. You are almost legendary.

SOREL. *(not pleased)* Almost?

EDWARD. What sort of cad would discuss his illicit affairs with his own wife? It's no wonder she shot him dead.

BRIDGIT. If she shot him.

ALICE. I am convinced I did precisely that.

VICTORIA. And my painting was the next victim in her vengeful spree.

ERIC. That painting deserved to be slain.

VICTORIA. Alice, hand me your pistol.

BRIDGIT. *(as ALICE reaches into her purse)* Leave it be. Now to the matter at hand –

VICTORIA. No one can fathom my agony! I will translate my anguish into art. *(She starts to sway.)*

BRIDGIT. I must hear in your own words what every one of you did when you left the room. It's time for a proper investigation.

SOREL. How delightful!

ALICE. Before we begin, might I have a spot of tea?

SOREL. The sun no longer has his hat on, dear. Won't you join us in a cocktail?

ALICE. I must keep my wits about me.

JACK. *(quickly, before BRIDGIT can object)* I'll take care of it, luv.

ERIC. And a tumbler of milk, if I may.

JACK. At your service. Back in a couple of jiffies.

(He exits into the kitchen.)

SOREL. Drinks, darling?

EDWARD. Brilliant.

(He heads for the bar trolley.)

VICTORIA. *(swaying more forcefully)* A new piece is

aborning. I shall call it, "Lament Macabre."

EDWARD. It sounds a barrel of monkeys.

(**SOREL** *puts the waltz record on the gramophone, and turns up the volume. There is chatter and hubbub.* **BRIDGIT** *watches everyone closely as:* **EDWARD** *pours and distributes drinks, then he and* **SOREL** *dance.* **VICTORIA** *dances around the room, mournfully.* **JACK** *returns from the kitchen with a tea tray, a glass of milk and a lager for himself.* **ALICE** *and* **ERIC** *prepare their tea. Everyone talks at once. The mood is festive and gay, except* **VICTORIA**'s *dance, which is funereal.* **BRIDGIT** *notices something and yanks the needle off the record. Everyone stops talking.* **BRIDGIT** *crosses to* **ALICE**.)

BRIDGIT. Alice, I see you're not wearing a wedding ring.

(*Everyone looks at* **ALICE**'s *ringless finger.*)

SOREL. I hadn't noticed.

EDWARD. I say, that's very good, Bridgit.

VICTORIA. (*joylessly*) The maid is psychic.

BRIDGIT. (*to* **ALICE**) Out with it, lass. Are ya married t' Mr. Pearce or are ya not?

ALICE. Not.

SOREL. But you said you were!

BRIDGIT. She said no such thing.

ALICE. All of you rushed the fences and assumed we were married.

EDWARD. Predictably, the pious Mr. Pearce was living in sin.

ERIC. Walter Pearce must have driven her to the brink. She looks innocent as a dove.

SOREL. There is a rather vague look about you, Alice – as if you've misplaced something.

ALICE. I have very poor eyesight, Mrs. Bennett. But I feel it is imprudent for me to be seen in public wearing my spectacles.

SOREL. Very wise. I would rather walk into walls than wear spectacles.

VICTORIA. Men look distinguished in eyeglasses. Women look morose.

ERIC. Are you suggesting that if a woman requires spectacles, she should walk round without them for the sake of vanity?

SOREL. Absolutely.

JACK. *(to* **ALICE***)* Put on your eyeglasses, Alice. You're among friends.

*(***ALICE*** removes a pair of gigantic spectacles from her handbag and puts them on. She looks at everyone, for the first time.* **VICTORIA** *and* **SOREL** *gasp in horror.)*

VICTORIA. They are truly hideous.

EDWARD. More binoculars.

JACK. But she can't see a thing without 'em.

VICTORIA. That is no justification for her to disfigure herself.

SOREL. She's seen all she needs to see. Take them off at once, Alice, and promise you will never don them again in this house.

*(***ALICE*** returns her eyeglasses to her purse.)*

EDWARD. Do you wear those spectacles when you attend the theatre?

ALICE. I've never been to the theatre.

EDWARD. Dear God! A life without theatre is a life not worth living.

JACK. I feel the same about sausages.

EDWARD. Alice, I would like to offer you a complimentary pair of tickets to *Daphne's Delight.*

ERIC. The poor girl has suffered enough.

BRIDGIT. *(to* **ALICE***)* When you tried to gun down Mr. Pearce, where were your spectacles?

ALICE. In my purse.

BRIDGIT. *(to everyone)* Do ya see that hole in the wall? Just there?

*(Everyone looks where **BRIDGIT** is pointing and indeed, there's a hole in the wall.)*

ERIC. *(poking his finger in the hole)* I feel the bullet with the tip of my finger. It's still warm.

ALICE. So I didn't hit my target?

EDWARD. Not by a long chalk, dear.

SOREL. Alice, I would suggest – and I say this against every instinct in my celebrated fashion sense – if you plan to shoot anyone else in future, put on your spectacles, at least for the moment.

ALICE. *(indicating her "purse")* But I wanted so to kill him. I packed all my belongings to take with me to prison.

SOREL. Mightn't you have had some of your wardrobe shipped to your destination? That's what I do when I travel.

ERIC. That remark betrays a profound misunderstanding of the criminal justice system.

ALICE. So I am entirely innocent? Oh, no!

*(**ALICE** bursts into tears, and wails loudly.)*

EDWARD. Alice, I beg you to find a less piercing method of coping with your failures.

BRIDGIT. *(to **ALICE**)* If you aren't his wife, why did you want him dead?

ALICE. Being married isn't the only reason to want to kill someone –

EDWARD. – although it is certainly the most customary.

ERIC. Wife or mistress, she failed utterly in her mission. If I were in her boots, I would be devastated – suicidal, even.

ALICE. Oh, no!

SOREL. Eric, you mustn't criticize dear Alice. We've been forced to witness the gruesome display of her wearing spectacles. How much degradation can a woman tolerate of an evening?

(**ALICE** *shrieks in grief.*)

EDWARD. Will you shut up!? (**ALICE** *stops crying instantly. A beat, then:*) I behaved with malice, Alice. I beg your pardon.

ERIC. Given that she botched her effort, shouldn't we consider natural causes?

SOREL. Bridgit has her heart set on solving a crime, Eric. We mustn't disappoint her.

BRIDGIT. (*ominously*) A murderer is amongst us!

ALICE. If I didn't kill Walter Pearce, who did, pray?

SOREL. We are all suspects! How enthralling. No one has ever suspected me of even the slightest infraction.

EDWARD. Save the *Daily Mail*.

SOREL. Edward, must you torment me? I demand another cocktail.

EDWARD. Would anyone fancy a drink? Victoria?

VICTORIA. Never! Alcohol interferes with my brainwaves. When I drink, I become entirely incoherent.

BRIDGIT. For our own safety, we must identify the culprit before he – or she – strikes again.

EDWARD. (*eagerly*) – and the room will be bristling with corpses.

VICTORIA. (*fearful of* **BRIDGIT**) Tonight, however, I shall have a martini. This is a special occasion.

JACK. Queer way to put it.

SOREL. I refuse to sit alongside this dead body a moment longer. I find his posture entirely unsuitable.

EDWARD. One thing we've all learned this evening – death is detrimental to poise of any sort.

JACK. Should I set 'im up straight?

VICTORIA. (*looking* **JACK** *in the eye*) Take him away, Jack. He is boring me.

JACK. Where to?

ALICE. The garden seems appropriate – amongst the flowers.

BRIDGIT. The body won't be leavin' this room. If ya don't want to look at him, put him in a chair and turn it round. *(to* JACK *and* ERIC*)* And go easy.

(JACK *and* ERIC *struggle as they place* WALTER *in a chair which they carry and face upstage.* WALTER*'s arms dangle over the sides.)*

ALICE. *(wondering where* WALTER *has been relocated)* Is he gone?

EDWARD. He is – upstage, as it were.

BRIDGIT. *(stops* ERIC *before he sits)* Alright, lad, where were you at the time of the murder?

ERIC. I was in the root cellar, whither you had assigned me.

BRIDGIT. Did ya stay put in the cellar till ya heard the gun?

ERIC. Yes, then I rushed upstairs to see what had happened.

EDWARD. That's a bit wide of the truth, Eric. I saw you enter this room moments before Mr. Pearce was shot.

BRIDGIT. Out with it – what were ya doing in here?

SOREL. *(to* ERIC, *flatteringly)* You wicked boy.

ERIC. I – I left something behind and came to retrieve it.

BRIDGIT. *(She pulls open* ERIC*'s jacket, and removes the knife from his inside pocket.)* Aha!

VICTORIA. Political murders are so dreary. I prefer crimes of passion.

SOREL. Isn't that the table knife I placed on Walter's tray, alongside his lettuce?

JACK. That knife couldn't cut an onion.

EDWARD. Suggesting that Eric did not pierce Mr. Pearce.

BRIDGIT. Not with that knife he didn't. Ya don't see any blood, do ya? All the same I won't be havin' any guest abscond with the cutlery. *(Glaring at* ERIC, *she puts the knife down.)*

ALICE. But Eric, why did you return upstairs if it wasn't to murder Mr. Pearce?

BRIDGIT. Anyone notice that the bookshelf is a wee sparse?

(Everyone looks at the bookcase, except **ALICE***, who looks around wondering where it is.)*

VICTORIA. *(to* **SOREL***)* This maid has a sixth sense.

EDWARD. *(rushing to the bookcase)* My library has been purloined!

BRIDGIT. To the cellar, Jack – and confiscate anything what don't belong there.

JACK. Okey dokey. *(He exits to the root cellar.)*

SOREL. *(moves in closer to* **ERIC***, then moves away suddenly)* Eric, after pedaling thirty-five miles, chasing Edward round the garden, and resting amongst the root vegetables, the time has come for you to bathe, as you have begun to emit a very curious odor.

BRIDGIT. None of the suspects will be drawin' a bath till I discover who the killer is.

*(***JACK*** reenters, carrying a huge picture book, hiding the cover.)*

JACK. Nothing out o' the ordinary down there, Bridgit – but this!

(Dramatically, **JACK** *holds up the book and turns it face-out. On the cover is a glamorous photograph of Gertrude Lawrence's face.* **SOREL** *screams.* **ERIC** *grabs the book, and clutches it.)*

ERIC. Gertrude Lawrence! *(falls to his knees, rapturous)* She is an enchantress!

EDWARD. In fact, Miss Lawrence is a rabid capitalist who demands exorbitant fees for her West End appearances. And what's worse – she demands rewrites.

ERIC. She deserves all the world has to offer!

EDWARD. I am thoroughly baffled. Miss Lawrence appears in exactly the type of plays that you insist I cease to write.

SOREL. Edward, how dare you secret away pictures of that minx in my home? *(to* **ERIC***)* And as for you, degenerate – the time has come for you to return to the asylum. I shall ring them up at once.

BRIDGIT. The line's been severed, m'am.

ERIC. Gertrude Lawrence is a goddess! May she feast on caviar and bathe in champagne and slumber on sable for all eternity!

VICTORIA. Unyielding political convictions – ha!

JACK. A man will do anything for the love of a lass.

ALICE. And a lass, for her man.

EDWARD. Eric, I saw you cross centerstage, directly to the sofa, when you entered this room.

BRIDGIT. *(to* **ERIC***)* What do ya say to that, lad? Were ya doin' harm to Mr. Pearce?

ERIC. Not at all. *(shamefully)* I needed to be sure he was asleep. If he had seen me with the picture book, I'd have been mortified.

EDWARD. Did you intend to return my book to the shelf where it belongs, or make off with it?

ERIC. I intended to spend a quiet evening alone, in the root cellar – just Miss Lawrence and I – until *(pointing at* **ALICE***) she* came along and ruined everything.

ALICE. Oh, no!

BRIDGIT. And what were ya fixin' t' do with the knife, lad?

ERIC. I hoped to find something to eat down there. A turnip, perhaps.

VICTORIA. This investigation is becoming increasingly banal.

SOREL. Indeed, all we have thus far is a deluded socialist harboring secret desires for an overpraised ham, and a half-blind teetotaler showing up from out of nowhere with a hideous handbag.

BRIDGIT. We've only just begun. Where were you, Miss Van Roth, when ya heard the shot?

SOREL. Victoria was with me in my boudoir the entire time, Bridgit. She is exonerated from guilt.

BRIDGIT. And when you were in the kitchen preparin' the

lettuce?

ERIC. I was in this room at that time, and though she is demonstrably capable of heinous behavior, Miss Von Wrath was not present.

VICTORIA. *Van Roth!*

(She takes off her earring and hurls it at ERIC.*)*

ERIC. Ow!

VICTORIA. A double martini, Edward.

*(*EDWARD *heads to the bar trolley.)*

SOREL. Victoria darling, at what point do you become incoherent?

VICTORIA. I have no idea – I am incoherent when it happens.

BRIDGIT. Did anyone see Miss Van Roth return to this room following her grand exit up the stairs?

ERIC. *(simultaneously)* I did not.

SOREL. *(simultaneously)* She stayed upstairs.

EDWARD. *(simultaneously)* Not I.

JACK. *(simultaneously)* No, m'am.

ALICE. *(simultaneously)* I arrived late.

BRIDGIT. Alright then – for now. Mr. B, where were you when ya heard the pistol shot?

EDWARD. I was having a bath.

JACK. Like 'e said.

SOREL. I heard the water running.

BRIDGIT. *(to* EDWARD*)* Yet your head is still smeared all over with slickum.

EDWARD. I use precisely the right amount of hair tonic, if you please.

ERIC. I fail to see what the amount of brilliantine Mr. Bennett applies has to do with this investigation.

BRIDGIT. Ay, ya ran a bath, but didn't take one. Very fishy, Mr. B.

EDWARD. You have found me out, Bridgit. I confess, as I

stand among you – *(everyone gasps)* – that I remain soiled from the events of the day.

ALICE. But why draw a bath when one has no intention of bathing?

BRIDGIT. So himself could use it as an alibi. But that headful of grease gave him away.

EDWARD. Bridgit, I would rather be drawn and quartered than suffer any further abuse regarding my personal grooming.

JACK. Did you know 'air tonic is made out of petroleum? If you're low on petrol when you're motorin' and 'ave a bottle with ya, just pour it in the tank and you're off!

EDWARD. I'll make note of that, Jack. Now may we quit the topic of hair care?

ERIC. The innocent do not require alibis, Mr Bennett.

SOREL. Are you guilty, Edward?

BRIDGIT. Mr. B, why were ya were peerin' into the room when Eric ventured up from below?

VICTORIA. How could you know that?

BRIDGIT. Himself said as much – *(to everyone)* – all of you heard him. *(to* **EDWARD***)* And when you showed up in Cookham this afternoon, why were ya fiddlin' with the bottles on the bar trolley?

EDWARD. I was entirely alone at the time.

VICTORIA. *(fearfully)* This maid is telepathic.

BRIDGIT. From the kitchen, I spied ya open a bottle and empty in somethin' from a vial.

SOREL. Edward, I cannot express my gratitude to you at this moment. I thought that our passion was extinct, only to discover that you have poisoned a man out of love for me.

(She throws herself into his arms.)

I adore you, darling. I promise to visit you every day in prison, wearing a black Schiaparelli hat with a sheer veil.

BRIDGIT. Don't lift ya hopes, Mrs. B. Mr. Bennett didn't kill anyone.

SOREL. I am bitterly disillusioned. Edward, another cocktail, at once.

EDWARD. Anyone else?

(He heads to the bar trolley.)

VICTORIA. I will not imbibe another drop until the maid reveals the exact bottle into which Edward emptied his vial.

BRIDGIT. *(picking up the bottle)* 'Twas the scotch.

VICTORIA. A double martini.

ERIC. *(to* **BRIDGIT***)* But I saw Mr. Pearce pour himself a drink from that bottle and quaff it down.

*(***EDWARD** *distributes the drinks.)*

BRIDGIT. It wasn't poison Mr. B poured in – 'twas a wee bit of sleeping draught. I recognized the vial.

SOREL. *(intrigued)* Is this so, Edward?

ALICE. Did you intend to put all of your guests into a coma?

EDWARD. I suspected that Sorel would be spending the week-end with – the remains. I wanted to be certain that at least one of them was sedated.

SOREL. *(intrigued)* The idea of me and Walter locked in embrace was so traumatic that you decided to tranquilize him?

EDWARD. Actually, it was you that I hoped to put under, darling. I thought it would be amusing if after a few drinks, Walter found you snoring like a bulldog.

SOREL. I do not snore. I have never snored in my life.

JACK. *(amused)* Beg pardon, Mrs. B, but I can hear you from outside.

BRIDGIT. *(sharing* **JACK***'s amusement)* Shatters the window panes, she does.

EDWARD. Your snoring is why I took up sleeping draughts

in the first place.

SOREL. I hardly suspected when we began this investigation that it would stoop to the level of malicious personal attacks. This is an outrage.

EDWARD. I must acknowledge that the deafening roar you make is accompanied by a slight whistle which I find utterly enchanting.

SOREL. Thank you, darling. Sit by me, will you? Alice, reluctant as I am to hurl you into the void, I'm afraid you must relocate.

(**ALICE** *stands, and begins to feel her way around the room.* **JACK** *guides her to a chair.*)

ERIC. The list of suspects is diminishing.

EDWARD. And the tension mounts.

SOREL. Intermittently, with frequent amusing interruptions.

ALICE. I've been travelling all day. Is there anything at all to eat? Scones, perhaps?

JACK. Only sardines and lettuce. Want some?

SOREL. Don't, Jack.

JACK. Why not, Mrs. B?

BRIDGIT. On account of the poison herbs?

VICTORIA. This maid is paranormal. (*holding up her empty glass*) I must drink!

(**EDWARD** *gets her a drink.*)

ERIC. Are you suggesting that Mrs. Bennett put poison herbs in the salad? What kind of home is this?

ALICE. My attempt to shoot Mr. Pearce turns out to have been only one among many violations perpetrated this evening.

ERIC. You served that salad to Walter Peace, and I watched as he consumed it. Sorel Bennett is the murderer!

SOREL. Murder*ess*, if you please.

ALICE. Mrs. Bennett, you are the last person I would have suspected.

SOREL. How very rude. Apparently, no one has ever considered me to be even the slightest threat. Well, now you are all the wiser. I am a murderess! I have poisoned Walter Pearce with garden greens!

VICTORIA. Brava!

JACK. Well done, Mrs. B.

EDWARD. *(amused)* "Murder by Roughage."

SOREL. Must you mock me, Edward? I at least accomplished my mission. You were unable to even medicate me into an afternoon nap.

BRIDGIT. Not so quick. All the herbs ya gathered weren't poison, m'am.

SOREL. Of course they were. There was black nightingale and hemlock and me and –

BRIDGIT. *(interrupting)* You mean yew.

SOREL. I harvested them, yes.

BRIDGIT. Along with arugula and mustard greens and watercress.

EDWARD. But Bridgit, you identified each herb alphabetically, and claimed they were poisonous.

JACK. 'Eard ya meself, luv.

BRIDGIT. 'Tis true – but 'twas a wee lie, ya see.

SOREL. Why on earth would you attempt to mislead us? We are your employers.

ERIC. You expect that to inoculate you – a couple who sully their liquor and toss poisonous salads?

BRIDGIT. Jack spilled the beans about the big row the two of ya had in town.

JACK. I cannot tell a lie.

BRIDGIT. Then Mr. B showed up and slipped the contents of his vial into the scotch. Next comes Mrs. B with a basket of suspicious greens. So I perjured meself, and claimed all of the herbs were poison. Then I threw away all of the dangerous herbs. Very naughty of you, Mrs. B.

SOREL. This week-end is a catastrophe. I invite the wrong man, and whilst the rest of us starve, he enjoys an appetizing salad.

EDWARD. Did you seriously intend to do away with me, Sorel?

SOREL. Truth be told, I was unaware that poison herbs might prove fatal. I had only hoped for you to become violently ill.

EDWARD. How very kind.

JACK. *(to* **SOREL***)* You could never poison anyone, m'am. You're too batty, if you don't mind me sayin'.

ERIC. Which implies, by process of elimination, that Jack is the murderer.

ALICE. Jack?

(Everyone looks at **JACK.** **VICTORIA***, quite tipsy, bursts out laughing.)*

ERIC. This is no time for euphoria, Victoria!

EDWARD. Brilliant, Eric, I must say.

ERIC. *(flattered)* Much obliged, Mr. Bennett.

JACK. She's all tanked up.

BRIDGIT. Miss Van Roth, how is it that when I turned on the lights, you were at the front door?

SOREL. Bridgit, this investigation is becoming tedious. We are all utterly exhausted. What say we –

BRIDGIT. *(interrupting)* What are ya tryin' to hide, Mrs. B?

SOREL. *(unconvincingly)* Nothing. Nothing at all.

EDWARD. That line-reading was entirely unconvincing.

SOREL. Hush, Edward. I'm not performing in one of your plays.

EDWARD. *(an idea occurs to him)* I'm beginning to think you could be...

BRIDGIT. Miss Van Roth, where is your scarf?

SOREL. *(quickly)* Upstairs, in my bedroom.

VICTORIA. Sorel, our friendship is boundless – cosmic. But

I will not permit you to prevaricate on my behalf. A double martini, Edward.

(**EDWARD** *heads to the bar trolley and mixes* **VICTORIA** *a drink.*)

VICTORIA. Maid, here is the intelligence you crave. Sorel implored me not to leave her room. She knew whither I was bound.

SOREL. Victoria, you musn't reveal all your secrets.

VICTORIA. Make it a triple, Edward, and I will divulge everything.

EDWARD. There is no such thing as a triple.

SOREL. *(to* **EDWARD***)* Then two doubles, at once. The sooner she becomes comatose, the better.

VICTORIA. I came down the stairs, passed through this room, and hurried outside.

EDWARD. *(hands* **VICTORIA** *a drink)* Out of doors? But nature goes against your very nature.

VICTORIA. I couldn't wait any longer. I had to see Jack. He is my boyfriend!

EDWARD/ERIC. Jack!?

BRIDGIT. You're jokin'!

SOREL. Victoria, I am livid. I struggled these many months to keep your love affair quiet, only to have you broadcast all in a drunken stupor.

VICTORIA. I am mad about the boy! I will shout it from the rooftops!

ALICE. Oh, no!

VICTORIA. Corroborate, Jack.

JACK. I met Victoria when I drove 'er 'ome from one of the Bennett's receptions. She was workin' in clay at the time – and asked me to pose for her.

BRIDGIT. Tell me you kept your skivvies on, lad.

JACK. *(shamefully)* Stripped down all the way.

VICTORIA. Jack has an extraordinary physique. The sculpture is on display at my studio, and has electrified all who have seen it. But no one knows it's the Bennett's chauffeur.

JACK. That's 'cause it looks like my Uncle Bob after 'e got run down by a lorry.

BRIDGIT. *(slaps the back of* **JACK***'s head)* Physiques are not meant for public display!

VICTORIA. From that night on, our love was uninhibited.

ERIC. Lust, you mean.

VICTORIA. That too. Together, we explored the depths and the heights. We were fervent – fanatical!

EDWARD. So you came to Cookham for further exploration of Jack's physique, and not to console my wife at all.

SOREL. Of course I knew from the moment she arrived – but how sweet of you to care, dear.

VICTORIA. Without Jack, I am an empty shell. A husk. A carcass.

*(***VICTORIA*** tries to stand, but she's wobbly.* **ALICE** *puts on her glasses.)*

ERIC. While intriguing from a class perspective, what does this forbidden love affair have to do with murder of Walter Pearce?

ALICE. Do you love her, Jack?

JACK. Not now, Alice.

ALICE. Tell me if you love her. I must know!

VICTORIA. Who are you, woman?

SOREL. Alice, is it absolutely necessary for you to sport those spectacles?

ALICE. It is essential. I must look Jack in the eye.

BRIDGIT. *(to* **ALICE***)* Are ya from Kent, dearie?

ALICE. However did you know?

BRIDGIT. So you're Jack's home-town lass.

ALICE. We've been sweethearts since the age of ten, haven't we Jack?

*(***JACK*** turns away.)*

SOREL. You journeyed all the way to Cookham to see your

Romeo? How romantic!

ALICE. Time was when Jack would come to Kent every month. *(glares at* **VICTORIA***)* But his visits have become less frequent of late.

SOREL. Oh, Edward, how I long for our starry-eyed youth.

EDWARD. – as we lurch into bleary-eyed middle age.

VICTORIA. Jack, you have annihilated me.

ALICE. It's me he loves! *(stands and approaches* **JACK***)* Tell them, Jack!

BRIDGIT. *(to* **JACK***)* I told ya, lad – too many lasses – that's askin' for trouble.

VICTORIA. There are more? Am I part of a – menagerie?

ALICE. No, Jack, no! Say it isn't so!

JACK. *(a beat, then)* I won't lie. I've 'ad plenty of women. Girl in every port – that's me nature. It's why I'm a single man – like I told ya, Mr. B. But I respect the ladies, and treat 'em kindly. And I never told any of 'em that they was the only one.

VICTORIA. I am reduced to nothingness. Oblivion.

ERIC. And I am thoroughly confused. Alice, if you came to Cookham to see Jack, why did you try to gun down Walter Pearce?

ALICE. I felt I must do something to earn back Jack's love. Mr. Pearce was not a good man. He did a terrible thing.

BRIDGIT. Are you in service to him, dearie?

ALICE. Have been, these fifteen years.

VICTORIA. The maid is omniscient! I surrender! *(wobbling over to* **ALICE***'s purse)* I vowed to do anything for you, Jack – and I've kept my promise.

ALICE. You've broken my heart, Jack.

*(***ALICE*** pulls at* **JACK***'s jacket, trying to force him to face her.)*

Look at me!

*(***VICTORIA*** takes the pistol from* **ALICE***'s handbag*

and shoots. ALICE *falls to the floor, and her glasses fall off.)*

VICTORIA. *(to* ALICE*)* Sorry, darling. I was aiming for him.

*(*VICTORIA *shoots again, and* JACK *jumps away. Then* VICTORIA *falls to the ground.* BRIDGIT *takes the gun.* JACK *rushes to* ALICE*, and checks to see if she's been shot, as* EDWARD *rushes to* VICTORIA*.)*

BRIDGIT. How is she, lad?

ERIC. Is she dead?

JACK. She's not dead – she's fainted.

SOREL. And Victoria?

EDWARD. Dead –

(Everyone gasps.)

– drunk.

ALICE. *(opening her eyes)* Jack? Is that you?

JACK. None other, luv.

ALICE. What has happened?

BRIDGIT. You've been shot, lass – but it's just a graze.

ALICE. *(noticing the wound)* Oh, dear. Perhaps I should dress my wound. Might I use the loo?

*(*JACK *helps* ALICE *to her feet, and guides her up the stairs.)*

ERIC. Bridgit, what in heaven's name is going on here? I beg you to explain.

EDWARD. *(with delight)* The plot has thickened considerably!

SOREL. *(genuinely intrigued)* Much more compelling than any of your recent efforts!

ERIC. I demand to know who killed Mr. Pearce.

JACK. *(from the top of the stairs)* It's time for me to 'ave my say.

*(*EDWARD, SOREL, *and* ERIC *sit, and* JACK *remains standing.* BRIDGIT *hovers near the chair where* WALTER *is seated.)*

Walter's folks lived on a fine estate in Kent. When me dad died in the war, mum moved us down there from the East End, to be in service to the Pearces. Alice and 'er mum worked for them too. Walter 'ad a weakness for the ladies, 'e did – and for drink. 'E came home one night, stinkin' to the gills. Lost 'is balance goin' up to 'is room, and knocked me mum down the stairs. Not on purpose – but the poor thing never recovered. The Pearces 'ushed up the entire affair – didn't want it known their fine young son was to blame. Pushed a few quid me way to keep me quiet. Walter never looked me in the eye again. I moved back to London when I got a bit older, and tried to put it out of me mind. Took jobs 'ere and there – then came in service for you, Mr. B. But I couldn't bury my loathin' for Walter Pearce. Then from out o' the blue this very day, Mrs. B says she invited the man 'oo caused the death of me mum.

ERIC. Is this a confession? Did you murder Walter Pearce for revenge?

BRIDGIT. *(quickly, before* JACK *can speak)* You told Miss Van Roth what Walter had done to your mum, am I right, Jack?

JACK. When I picked 'er up at the station.

BRIDGIT. Ladies and gentlemen, hold onto your hats. Now comes the answer you've all been waitin' for. 'Twas Victoria Van Roth who murdered Walter Pearce.

SOREL. Victoria!?

BRIDGIT. Strangled him with her scarf, she did. There are red marks to prove it, all round his neck.

JACK. Bridgit, you don't –

BRIDGIT. *(interrupting)* I know, lad. Victoria didn't let you in on was what she was plannin'. She sneaked down to this room, wrapped the scarf round Walter's neck and choked the life out of him. Then she ran outside to tell you. Must have hidden the scarf somewhere out there.

JACK. It's in the Bentley.

ERIC. Well, I for one am not in the least surprised.

SOREL. My dearest friend is a murderess. *(proudly)* I knew she was capable of great achievement.

EDWARD. Pity she's immobilized, and unable to receive your acclaim.

ERIC. You are both utterly delusional.

SOREL. Yes, Eric, we know. Isn't it divine?

EDWARD. Jack, I am astonished that two women, worlds apart, would go to such lengths for your love.

BRIDGIT. Always had a way with the ladies, Jack has.

EDWARD. I am sorely envious. Sorel, would you ever kill on my behalf?

SOREL. I limit my brutality to hurling the occasional vase.

EDWARD. Darling – an idea has been stirring, prompted by tonight's events. I believe I have the play!

SOREL. Edward, has this week-end served as inspiration?

EDWARD. *(discovering this moment)* I believe it has!

SOREL. Then murder and all, it was entirely worthwhile!

ERIC. I find it extremely distasteful for the two of you to carry on about your careers whilst the body of your strangled guest has yet to be removed.

SOREL. Eric, need I remind you that not a one of these guests was invited?

EDWARD. Come, Sorel. *(takes her hand and leads her upstairs)* I will tell you about my new play. It will be called *Death by Design*.

SOREL. *(eagerly)* Tell me, darling – am I murdered, or am I the murderess?

EDWARD. You will hear all from the very first scene, where the chauffer and the maid engage in seemingly idle banter, which in truth holds the key to the entire plot.

SOREL. I beg of you, Edward – I must know this one thing. Do I die in the end?

EDWARD. You, my dear, will suffer a spectacular death, the likes of which has never been seen on the London stage!

SOREL. *(rapturously)* I am over the moon! I never doubted you for a moment, darling.

EDWARD. There's my girl.

(They kiss, and full of excitement, exit up the stairs hand in hand.)

ERIC. I am convinced that Edward and Sorel Bennett are the most narcissistic, egotistical, self-absorbed couple in England. I'll have nothing more to do with them. *(He stands, and prepares to leave.)*

JACK. Pushin' off?

ERIC. I'm bicycling back to London at once.

BRIDGIT. Wait till daylight, lad.

ERIC. I cannot tolerate another minute in this house, thank you very much. *(crosses to door)* I say, it's high time you rang up the Inspector.

BRIDGIT. *(looking around)* Don't fancy that anybody will be leaving any time soon. *(picks up the book)* Here's the picture book, lad. Mrs. Bennett would want ya to take it.

ERIC. *(grabs the book)* Since Mr. Pearce won't be needing it, might I spend the night in Caligula room?

(BRIDGIT nods, and ERIC hurries upstairs. JACK and BRIDGIT sit on the sofa.)

JACK. Bridgit, I'm an 'onest man. I would never mislead you or lie to you.

BRIDGIT. The marks on Mr. Pearce's neck were made by a strong man's hands.

JACK. *(looks her in the eye)* Soon as 'e was alone, I crept in and snapped 'is neck in one quick move.

BRIDGIT. Miss Van Roth had no idea what you'd done when she wrapped her scarf around him.

JACK. When I told 'er 'bout Walter and me mum, she said, "Leave it to me." Never entered me mind she'd try to finish 'im off.

BRIDGIT. I'm through with the Tittle Tattle. I don't want t' be readin' no more about murders. Had enough of that business, I have.

JACK. I best be callin' the Doctor and Inspector Benson.

BRIDGIT. Not with that telephone you won't.

JACK. 'Oo was it severed the wire? *(realizing)* Bridgit!

BRIDGIT. I wanted to solve a crime, Jack – all on me own.

JACK. But it's not proper for Victoria to get the blame for somethin' I done.

BRIDGIT. She won't, Jack. Depend on it.

JACK. Why won't she? What ya mean?

*(Suddenly **ALICE**, with a bandage on her wound, comes tumbling down the stairs. **JACK** rushes to her.)*

ALICE. My apologies, Jack. I've caused you so much trouble tonight.

JACK. Not to worry, luv. I know that what you did – what you tried to do, you did for me.

BRIDGIT. *(to **ALICE**)* You acted out of true love, dearie. A caring lass, you are.

ALICE. *(looking around)* Whatever's become of my handbag and spectacles?

*(**JACK** picks up **ALICE**'s glasses and puts them on her.)*

JACK 'Ere you go. You look loverly.

*(**JACK** and **ALICE** smile and kiss.)*

BRIDGIT. Why don't you spend the night with us here in Cookham, Alice? *(indicating **VICTORIA**)* There's a spare room.

ALICE. That's awfully kind.

*(**JACK** picks up **ALICE**'s handbag, and they head upstairs together. Suddenly, **WALTER** begins snoring loudly. **BRIDGIT** registers no surprise.*

After a moment, she walks over and pokes him).

BRIDGIT. Rise and shine, Mr. Pearce.

WALTER. *(stands and rubs the sleep from his eyes)* What time is it?

BRIDGIT. Past your bedtime.

WALTER. Was I napping? I feel surprisingly well-rested.

BRIDGIT. You missed all the excitement.

WALTER. I would like a lift to the station at once.

BRIDGIT. Like I told ya, the last train left hours ago. And the Caligula room is occupied. You'll have to spend the night in the root cellar. *(pointing to the kitchen door)* It's through there.

WALTER. You are without a doubt the most impudent maid in the entire history of the British Empire.

BRIDGIT. Much obliged, sir.

(**WALTER** *notices* **VICTORIA** *on the floor. Startled, he walks over and kicks her gently. She comes to, sits up and sees him standing over her.)*

VICTORIA. Wall is – resurrected!

(**VICTORIA** *faints, falling back to the floor.* **JACK** *appears on the stairway.)*

JACK. *(delighted)* Mr. Pearce! You're alive!

WALTER. Of course I'm alive. And I consider myself lucky, having spent the evening among such depraved company.

BRIDGIT. You have no idea how lucky, sir.

(**WALTER** *exits out the kitchen door.)*

JACK. Bridgit, you knew all along he was alive! You're a wily devil, you are!

(**JACK** *picks* **BRIDGIT** *up and she squeals with delight.)*

(THE CURTAIN CRASHES DOWN.)

THE END

WHAT THE CRITICS ARE SAYING ABOUT
DEATH BY DESIGN

"Rob Urbinati's *Death by Design* is a wildly funny comedy that's exquisitely crafted in the style of British playwright Noel Coward with a major added fillip: an Agatha Christie-style whodunit murder mystery. [...] *Death by Design* is intentionally written in Coward's style, complete with interesting, over-drawn characters, brilliant comic repartee and wonderfully incisive social commentary. Plus there's the Agatha Christie element: a country estate full of mysterious guests and isolated by a snipped telephone wire. *Death by Design* is definitely a major must-see."
– The Forecaster

"These characters have some great lines to deliver, particularly (of course) playwright Edward, in whose mouth the snarky urbanities are like whiskeyed butter. Playwright Urbinati gives him and the others a fun array of verbal flourishes – rhymed character names are an ongoing gag – and the conversation takes some entertaining digs at theater itself, as well as the archetypes of the British class system. And oh, yes, the murder. Of course it's less a mortal emergency than a vehicle for everyone's lampoonery, especially once they've drained the brandy and moved on to gin."
–The Portland Phoenix

Ingram Content Group UK Ltd.
Milton Keynes UK
UKHW021814160723
425226UK00009B/57

9 780573 700934